Virgin

And the

Hunter

Matthew cash

Copyright Matthew Cash Burdizzo Books 2016.

Edited by Matthew Cash, Burdizzo Books. All rights reserved. No part of this book may be reproduced in any form or by any means, except by inclusion of brief quotations in a review, without permission in writing from the publisher.

Each author retains copyright of their own individual story. This book is a work of fiction. The characters and situations in this book are imaginary. No resemblance is intended between these characters and any persons, living, dead, or undead. This book is sold subject to the condition that it shall not, by way of trade or otherwise, be lent, resold, hired out or otherwise circulated without the publisher's prior consent in any form or binding or cover other than that in which it is published and without similar condition including this condition being imposed on the subsequent purchaser

Published in Great Britain in 2016 by Matthew Cash, Burdizzo Books Walsall, UK

PROLOGUE

Gothfuck Goddard, Greebo Goddard, Greedy Goddard, bastard, fucking freak, fucking fuck, fucking fucker, fat fucking freak, fat bastard, fat wanker, shit-stabbing shit sucker, wank-face, mother-fucking vampire, and cunt.

All these things have been hurled at me verbally in my twenty-one years on this earth. Numerous others have escaped my memory or have been locked away in some dark corner waiting to pounce on me, waiting to dig their sharp talons into my chest and remind me of the pain they once caused and are capable of causing once again. *(Some people accuse me of being 'over-dramatic'.)*

My name is Robert Goddard, but my friends call me 'God' *(this was not of my choosing)*

I am used to name-calling, as I've said; I've grown used to it over the years. I'm not going to portray this as a sob-story; I don't want you to feel sorry for me. Sure, I was bullied for a bit, but it was nothing that serious. You hear stories of children hanging themselves at the age of twelve because they couldn't stand being bullied any longer and saw no way out other than to put a rope around their neck. I never got bullied that much. It never got violent when I was a kid; just the odd jibe about being overweight at least once a day. I got used to it. As I grew older and started high school, the taunting became less frequent, but it was always there. A select few, when stuck for want of anything else to do, would occupy themselves with me if I was in the vicinity until the next period started. As I was overweight, obviously that would be the main topic of ridicule.

"Goddard, why are you so fat?" "What do you eat?" "Why don't you go on a diet?" The main leader of the select few would then grab my bitch-tits whilst his mates laughed. Luckily, the teachers, who were probably bullies when they were at school, would turn up then. They wouldn't say anything, they wouldn't need to. It would stop then.

As I grew older and my body didn't look so grossly overweight, I gained something I never had before. Confidence. I grew confident. I left school and joined Art College, where I was able to show my real self for once. I could wear what I wanted, do what I wanted and was able to make new friends.

No longer did I feel like I had to dress like everyone else so they wouldn't have something extra to mock me for. I used to walk around college, with badly dyed black and blonde hair in my eyes, listening to my Walkman. My Walkman was ever familiar with the likes of The Sensational Alex Harvey Band, Black Sabbath, The Clash, and almost anything really. I constantly wore ripped jeans and an oversized black and white stripy jumper that reminded me of the ones I'd seen Alex Harvey wear in pictures. Due to my musical influences and my array of piercings, nose, lip, and ear, I soon was welcomed into a small group of kids in the 'alternative' scene. Our group ranged from goth to punk, our goth, reluctantly named Kevin and got everybody to call him Nivek as it sounded a lot better than 'Kevin' and made him sound like he came from Poland or Russia, was forever decked-out in the blackest of blacks. Long black hair fell over ludicrously skinny cheekbones which were always hidden beneath the pale make-up he wore. He was heavily influenced by the mighty Marilyn Manson.

Thys pronounced Tice, short for Matteis, was from Italy; he suffered quite a bit of taunting purely for that alone. Another black-haired Manson fan, but no amount of makeup could tarnish his tanned-skin. Death metal was big in Italy, and Thys was one of the college's biggest importers of Italian metal. He wasn't forever in black, but was forever in blue T-shirts with the well-known, (if you're Italian maybe,) Italian death-metal band, 'Bastard Saints' on it.

The other member of our 'family' was Persephone, the only girl, who I developed a crush for from the moment I set eyes upon her. She was a sweet girl beneath a vibrant shock of red hair. When she smiled, it brought warmth to my soul, and she had kind blue eyes and was my closest friend.

Even though we were still social outcasts and misfits, life at the college was relatively peaceful. It was amazing how mature some of the other kids were, even though they were only a year older than they were when they had ripped the shit out of people like us. I don't think people even noticed us, which was exactly what we wanted.

We weren't your stereotypical goth-teens, obsessed with hating everything—our parents, our college, our lives. We didn't self-harm. Most of us had decent backgrounds.

Thys lived with his parents on the outskirts of town in a massive house. His dad worked for some big insurance firm in town and earned about £150,000 a year, so he had a weekly allowance on top of his grant, which meant that he was usually the drinks-dispenser when we went to the park on Friday afternoons. For some reason, he was the only one who the local off-licence would serve.

Persephone lived in a two-bedroom flat in town with her mother, who was like a twenty-year older version of her daughter. She had no known father, as her mother and she had disowned him when she was twelve years old, for reasons that Seph never went into.

Nivek was the offspring of a pair of absolute tits. His father was a stereotypical homophobic factory owner, who was certain his son was gay. Make-up + men = HOMOSEXUALITY. His mother sat at a supermarket checkout counter and gossiped all day. She knew more about the lives of her fellow colleagues than her own son.

What about me?

I lived in a village about nine miles from town, with my family. They were neither rich nor poor. My father was a landscape gardener, and my mother was a nurse. They took me for who I was and never commented on anything I wore or listened to unless they liked something. Often I would ask my mother or father whether they liked a particular t-shirt or song I was listening to, and they'd voice their opinions, whether positive or not. The older I got, the more independent I became and spent more and more time in the town. There was nothing of interest for me in my village.

At college, the four of us were so close that we decided to look for some student accommodation to live in. Thys' father gave us a bit of money to bide us time to look for jobs. We landed ourselves a four-bedroom house, ten minutes from college for quite reasonable rent. The area was a bit rough, but we were ecstatic that we had our own place. I was the first to find a job. I worked in the same supermarket as Nivek's mum. That was a real pain in the arse. Nivek's mum was a fucking bitch. Common as they come. Whenever she saw me, she'd make snide comments about my hair, or about me turning her son gay. She was a popular lady there, basically because, unfortunately for Nivek, she was rumoured to put it about a bit. All the older men always hung about her, hoping to have a go on the Supermarket Bike. They joined in with her teasing sometimes, but I was all 'grown up'. I could deal with 'harmless banter', as the manager had put it. Most of the time, I ignored the comments, now and again I'd say something back. They were all brain-dead anyway. Most of the staff had no ambitions; they had been there for twenty years. Don't get me wrong, I've nothing against supermarket workers or any type of workers. It's just, I can't abide ignorant people. People who just don't seem physically capable of learning new things, or accepting things that are 'different'.

I hate a lot of things in life, even though I'm contradicting what I said earlier about our group not hating everything. At nights, after we had got in from our jobs, we'd spend the first hour or so just ranting and raving about the things that had pissed us off each day. It was good therapy.

We all managed to find jobs. Seph worked in a pub called, The Drum and Monkey, a rock pub that had live bands on all the time. I was dead-jealous, even though there were a couple of staff members who were right bastards and referred to Seph as 'The Dyke' behind her back. What was it with some people? A guy wears make-up, he's gay. A girl has a nose ring and walks round in camouflage combats and band t-shirts and she's a lesbian.

Nivek, also a lucky bastard, refused to apply for the job vacancy at the supermarket and landed himself a place at HMV, the git.

As for Thys, his dad got him a few hours with the insurance company that he worked for, and of course, helped him out whenever he needed funds for whatever reason.

So that's how we spent our first few years at college. When the opportunity came, we'd be down at The Drum and Monkey having a few drinks, or we'd hang out in Christchurch Park until it got dark, and then go home to do college stuff. Even though I personally struggled a bit financially, life was good then, carefree. Things kind of went downhill from the moment I started killing people.

CHAPTER ONE

Let me first give you an idea of where I am writing this. I am sitting in a ridiculously cheap bed and breakfast in Zeebrugge. For those of you whose geography is lacking, that's in Belgium. The walls have hideous orange-and-brown wallpaper that looks as though it went out of fashion before the wallpaper paste dried. I am sprawled out on a double-bed that has an orange blanket, to match the walls. Cheap looking flat-packed furniture that I don't trust sits cautiously around the room as if they are expecting to be broken at any moment. The chest of drawers looks as though it is bracing itself for my attack. I am wearing baggy jeans that are cut off below the knee and a tattered and an oversized black and white striped jumper. My hair, which is blonde and black, has grown far too long, and it is somehow being contained by a simple elastic band. In front of me is the notebook I am writing this in, a selection of free pens that I acquired over the past few days, a large packet of aspirins, and my Stanley knife, it would have been a razor blade, but where the fuck do you actually buy them from? Do they have them in specialist shops, purely for wannabe suicides? But they are for later. I have a story to tell first.

Have you ever heard a piece of music that is so good it makes your face tingle? A piece of music that, when you hear it, you don't care if you go stone-deaf afterwards? A song that whenever you hear it, you must stop everything you are doing and concentrate one-hundred percent upon the melody and lyrics? Well, almost every song by Alex Harvey has that effect upon me. The rough-gruffness of his voice is so distinguishable, it makes me shudder. It also makes me wish I'd been born twenty years sooner so that I could have been at one of his concerts. I love the rawness of his songs, the lyrics and his hard Glaswegian accent. The legend died from a heart-attack in 1982, three years before I was born. Why are all the greatest musicians those who have died young? Would they still be known as the 'greatest' if they hadn't died at the peaks of their career? Is the main reason for them to be called 'the greatest' because they died before they managed to go to shit? Look at artists like The Rolling Stones, a globally famous band, but the songs people are interested in are over twenty-five years old. If a couple of the band members had died in 1980, would they be even bigger now than they are? The same goes for the likes of David Bowie and, dare I say it, Bob Dylan. Even though they are still reeling off albums every now and then, people only remember songs that are over twenty years old.

I wonder if any of 'the greatest' had survived, would their music have improved, or would they have fallen into the same trap? If Marc Bolan had decided not to go out for a drive that day and if Mark Chapman had decided that he'd not kill John Lennon, would they still be making unbelievable music now? When musicians reach their peak, should they stop there and then? How do they know they are at their peak?

I believe we all have our 'best before' date, and I believe mine is overdue. I've started the landslide down; I've reached my peak. My work prior to this date will be remembered more than what happens to me tomorrow and the day after. I think I reached my peak a little over two years ago.

It had been a glorious, sunny day and we'd all finished college at the same time. The four of us had been sitting in a quiet corner of Christchurch Park. Thys had treated us to a crate of cheap, French lager and we stretched out and discussed the ways of the world. Nivek, looking as pale as ever, admitted that summertime was the hardest time of the year to be a Goth. The black clothes absorbed the heat like a sponge does water. He believed that's why most Goths will say they love the winter.

Even though he liked to drink spirits, mainly for show, pint glasses didn't suit his style; he happily partook in the free-alcohol. Thys was making us all look anaemic by removing his T-shirt to show off his permanently tanned skin. Seph just lay still behind the biggest, darkest, ugliest sunglasses I'd ever seen. They were so hideous that they had gone beyond hideous and were cool.

Whether I was the only one to think it, I don't know, but she looked so cute. She had gained a new bout of confidence after, what must have seemed like decades, her dentist had removed her braces, revealing the prettiest teeth I'd seen. Without the brace, she smiled more and didn't have the usual morose expression upon her face. Plus, something that I was secretly jealous of was that I had begun to notice blokes look at her. She was like a flower, about to blossom. My crush on her increased with every breath she breathed and every smile she smiled. Often, she'd catch me staring off into space and wave a hand in front of my face. Little did she know that I was thinking of her.

Anyway, the sun was blazing down upon us, and seeing as it was a weekday, it was pretty deserted. We had walked up the steep, concrete road that leads through the park past the pond, with its fountain and three ducks. Through the children's play area, with its precautious bark chippings giving it a cushioned texture. The little wooden horses in a desperate need for a new coat of paint, the dilapidated red ball-shaped roundabout, plastered with graffiti and rust. We found our usual spot upon a mammoth monument that commemorated the people of our town who died during the Second World War. It was a big, ugly concrete platform, upon which stood a proud three-sided marble plinth. Favouring this to the grass, we sprawled out on the hot, concrete surface. I had taken off my rucksack and used it as a makeshift pillow, the others doing similar. Thys had opened the lagers, and we just drank and enjoyed one another's conversation. I don't know when it happened, but I had drifted off to sleep. I guess with the lager and the sun beating down on me I had naturally shut my eyes.

When I awoke, I was alone; I sat up looking about myself. The others had cleaned up and gone. I looked at the concrete where I lay and chuckled. Someone, Thys most probably, had drawn a chalk outline around me. How many people must have walked past and seen me lying there like the victim in a murder scene? I don't know what the time was, but judging by the sun, not that I'm an expert, of course, I'd guess it was early evening. I heard the faint sound of Led Zeppelin's, "Whole Lotta Love" coming from my mobile phone. I started to ferret through my rucksack to try and answer the damn thing, absentmindedly fiddling my tongue with my lip ring—A habit of mine. I found the phone and felt my face tingle when I saw Seph's name on the little, yellow screen. I pressed the thing to my ear, the phone hot from where my head lay. "Hello?" I said as I watched a couple in business suits stroll past, probably a shortcut on their way home.

"Hey babe, I hope by now you've seen Thys's interpretation of humour." It was Seph. I loved her voice.

"No, I only found out about it when I woke up inside the fucking morgue!" I said, sounding serious, but knowing she'd detect, as always, the thin edge of humour in my voice.

Seph laughed loudly through the phone. I loved hearing her laugh too. It was so mischievous. "Well, if it were up to the guys, they'd have left you there all night, but fortunately for you, they're scared of me, and I've made them wait with me, for you, at the entrance. See you in a bit?"

I sighed, secretly happy that they had waited for me. It took about ten minutes to walk to the other end of the park. I put my phone in my pocket and stood up. Looking down at the chalk outline, I tittered and made myself a mental reminder to come back before class the next day to wipe it off of the monument. I swung my bag over my shoulders and spun round to be greeted by a punch to the face. I don't know whether it was the force of the blow or the fact that I'd been caught unawares, but I fell backwards, hitting my head hard on the marble plinth. As I slid down the plinth, my nose was an explosion of pain and blood ran into my mouth. I made out two blokes, who looked a few years older than me, standing over me. I think I pleaded as they moved towards me.

"Give me your wallet." One of them said, he wore a dark-blue Reebok jumper and white tracksuit bottoms, had an acne-ridden face, and wore two gold earrings.

I was about to tell him that it was in my bag and began to sit forward, as my bag was trapped between my back and the plinth, but as soon as I moved, he set upon me again.

He yanked me by the hair away from the plinth and punched me in the back of the head. I sat forward, cradling my head in my hands, understandably, crying like a baby. The men started pulling at my rucksack, and, as they weren't too bright, they didn't realise that in the position I was in, it was going to be difficult to remove my bag. One of them tugged and tugged at my bag, half dragging me off the concrete platform, while the other attempted to force my arms into positions they really weren't capable of. With each failure of removing my bag, I received more blows—mostly kicks and stomping to my legs and lower torso.

Finally, I thought, through tears, blood, and snot, as they managed to get the bag from me. I thought they'd leave me then, seeing as they had what they wanted, but hell no. The acne-sufferer, who I think was the leader, started repeatedly kicking me in the stomach, alternating with his friend, who delivered kicks to my flying-hands. I felt one of my fingers snap immediately, so I did my best to clench my fists as much as possible. After a few moments, the rhythmic beating began to hurt less and less. In my last glimpse before a blood-spotted white Reebok trainer kicked me hard in the face ripping out my lip-piercing, knocking out three of my teeth, breaking my nose and a cheekbone, and sending me into oblivion, I saw acne-man withdraw a flick knife.

I knew my life was over.

CHAPTER TWO

You know when I awoke and saw the bright light, I honestly thought I had died and I was in a transcendental realm. I was wrong. The intense, searing pain that raged through my body reassured me that I was alive. As my vision became clearer, I could make out a bright-white strip-light above me. My eyes ached, and my eyelids felt as though they had been injected with fluid—I could barely open them. The face of an Indian doctor, of indeterminable age, appeared between the pink slits of my vision. He smiled sympathetically and said loud and clear, "Robert? Can you hear me?"

Of course I can, I thought, happy that, not only did my ears still work but also that I was still capable of intelligent thought, something that my two assailants lacked. I don't think I managed a perfectly decipherable 'yes', but the noise I made was a pretty good impersonation of one. The doctor shone a light into my eyes and did some other doctor-things that made him look like he knew what he was doing. He was waffling on about what had happened to me, where I was found, who by, and what he was doing like I was actually going to take it in and listen. Once he had given me the once-over, he left a nurse with me to prepare me for an x-ray.

X-ray gone and done, I was told that I had four cracked ribs, three lost teeth, one fractured cheekbone, one broken finger, and a partridge in a fucking pear tree. No internal bleeding and, surprisingly, no stab wounds. I felt sure in my last vision of my ordeal I had seen the acne-faced motherfucker get out a knife. However, no stab wounds. What was it the friendly Indian doctor had said to me in that jovial accent of his? Oh yes, that's it, "It could have been a lot worse." Oh, that's okay then! Thank you, Mister Muggermen, for not actually killing me, or giving me any long-term physical damage!

When I was capable of it, I chuckled for ages in the hospital bed when I came to the realisation that all the fucker's who jumped me would have gotten out of my bag was a few half full bottles of paint, a paint-splattered shirt, and bits of crap. I was slightly bemused that I was certain my wallet was in the bag too. If I had realised it wasn't in my pocket, it may've saved me the kicking.

You see, some might think that I should be angry that I had seven shades of shit beaten out of me for some paint, but I'm not. Yes, I'm angry that I was a victim of something that happens millions of times a day, all over the world, to millions of different people, and by the synchronisation of the two who did me; I would say they've done it before. The rhythmic kicking, surely if it were the first attack, they would get in one another's way. They obviously need more experience with getting rucksacks off of people though. I wonder what goes through a person's head at a time like that. Having someone powerless against you. You have control over how much you want to hurt them, of whether to keep on kicking and punching until they stop breathing or not. What goes through the person's mind whilst they see defenceless people's faces open up, noses explode, and teeth shatter beneath their force?

My parents had been with me all the previous evening, but I faked sleep to avoid the barrage of questions. They would have their answers in my time.

The morning after I was attacked, my friends came to the hospital. I don't know who was more shocked when they came into my ward, me or them. Nivek was the first to come in, and I hardly recognised him. He wore no black or white make-up and was wearing just plain, blue jeans, a plain black T-shirt and a look of horror on his face. Seph followed him, hand up to her face, tears in her eyes, lost for words. Thys joined them after a few seconds, his expression one of intense guilt. We didn't say anything for at least a minute, they just gathered around the bed. Nivek, who I think was back to being 'Kevin' for that day, slouched forward in the green armchair that festered beside the bed; Thys chose a hard wooden chair. Much to my delight, my dear Seph perched upon the side of the bed, head down, studying her chipped-purple nail varnish. My mouth didn't hurt as much anymore, even though I needed three stitches where my lip ring had been ripped out. I seemed like the only one capable of speech, and so I spoke first.

"God, what a bunch of miserable fuckers!"

Nivek risked a peek, but soon looked away and put his hands over his face muttering something indecipherable. Thys let loose a tear, which he wiped away immediately with a light-brown hand. Seph clutched the hand that wasn't bandaged and looked at me in my puffy eyes, tears welling up in hers. It was all the comfort I needed—her holding my hand. This first compassionate physical connection was almost worth being beaten to a bloody pulp. They sat, and I lay that way for the best part of thirty minutes, Nivek and Thys stealing glances, Seph caressing my hand with her soft touch.

The silence was finally broken by Thys, who made everyone in the ward jump by blurting out, "I'm sorry God!" before bursting out of the nearest door sobbing. Nivek ran after him.

Startled by this, I asked Seph what was going on.

Seph said, "I thought it was obvious. It was Thys' idea… Leaving you alone."

"I'm almost twenty-one Seph, I can be left alone, you know. Plus, it was only early evening." I said defending Thys. "It's no one's fault, but the two pricks who set upon me; you know we're always playing stupid jokes on each other. Remember when Thys fell asleep on the train back from V fest, and we drew a great big fuck off Poirot moustache on him? He walked around like that for hours, even down to the pub."

Seph snorted for a second, but then stopped, "But we never left him."

"So? That's not the point. Those guys could have just as easily jumped me when I was coming home from work. I was at the wrong time and place. I don't blame any of you."

She smiled weakly and squeezed my hand tighter, "Are you going to be okay?"

The smirk I attempted hurt, so I gave in. "I think so. It's mainly bruises and a few cracked bones."

"How many?" she asked, concerned.

"A few ribs, but everyone has cracked ribs, my cheekbone, umm... my finger, but that'll be okay unless I want to get married in the near future, and obviously, my nose."

"Oh, Jesus." She said gasping. "Does the doctor know how long you should take to heal?"

I shook my head. "He told me, but I wasn't really listening. The cracked stuff will probably give me gip for a few months, but I'll be okay. Could've been worse."

Seph still looked doubtful. "You're so brave."

I tried to do my best impression of a poor little injured soldier, "I'm alive; I'll be okay. Besides, this just means I'll have a few weeks off, which is great, I can finally get round to categorising my clothes and my vast collection of Russian pornography."

That got a laugh, a proper Seph laugh, and that sound itself had miraculous healing powers.

A little later, Nivek and a pale Thys turned up, and I told them pretty much the same thing. Thys left with more of his usual complexion, but I still felt as though he was blaming himself. Whilst they were there, they filled me in on what I had missed the previous night. Apparently, no one knows what or who disturbed the men, but my three amigos had given up waiting for me and had decided to come and meet me. On their way, they saw the two men who foolishly were walking about with my backpack, which was pretty distinctive, a light green/grey colour emblazoned with my favourite bands. The backpack was spotted with red, as were the trousers of one of the men. Unfortunately for me, as I couldn't provide an adequate description for the police, they saw the men from behind.

Upon seeing this, they bolted up to the monument where they found me. Thys had turned to run back after the two men, even though each one of them was twice as big as him, but the other two had restrained him and phoned an ambulance. Apparently, my little incident caused such a stir that Seph told a semi-circle of onlookers to 'fucking fuck off'. I was amazed to hear that there were onlookers; however, there almost always is. There are certain people who, when they hear an ambulance, they rush to the accident scene and stare with other sad morbid people. They always turn up. The remark that triggered off Seph's outburst was that some 'fat old cunt', her words not mine, said, a bit too loudly, to her equally 'fat old cunt' of a husband, "Hmmph, most probably to do with drugs."

And I was out cold for about ten minutes. I don't actually remember anything before being inside the hospital, but apparently, I was gurgling something about my artwork. At the time, I did not realise what I could have meant by that. I had trouble sleeping because of twinges here and there that the painkillers couldn't reach, and even though I was in a room full of other people whose ages ranged from around twelve to twenty-five, I felt so alone. It was whilst I was laying there on my second evening in the hospital; I remembered exactly which piece of artwork had been in my bag.

CHAPTER THREE

I had done a portrait of Seph one afternoon, from memory; I needed no photo. The piece was very good, even if I do say so myself, and I think I captured her beautifully. It just showed her looking out of the picture with her startling smile shining out, and her blue eyes staring out, almost hypnotically. As I created the shape of her cheekbones, I imagined actually being able to put my hand on her face to feel the bone structure, to feel the softness of her pale skin. Her red hair cascaded down over her naked shoulders.

I would've painted more. Actually, 'painted' is not the right word, as it was in pastel. However, as I can't think of a suitable substitute, I shall stick with 'painted'. I would've painted more of her, but much to my disappointment I had only seen that much of her. It was one of the most erotic things I have ever witnessed, when she came out of the bathroom at our house once with just a towel on, hiding her dignity. I think she thought she had the place to herself and was not expecting to find me sitting in the living-room. As soon as she saw me, her face flushed, almost as red as her fiery hair and she hollered, "shut your fucking eyes!" and ran through the room to the safety of her bedroom.

But it was already too late, for the glimpse I got was forever burned in my memory's hard drive. The sight of her curvaceous white thighs… Well, there's no need to go into that, let's just say that being a virgin myself, then and seeing that much of a young woman, in the flesh, so to speak, left me embarrassed and majorly turned on for hours, well days, afterwards. I don't think I faced her until later that evening when Nivek and Thys confronted me in front of Seph and asked me why I hadn't said anything to her all evening. I had denied it, but then Seph told them what happened, much to their amusement. They said the only way it could be rectified was if I was to go to the bathroom and come back into the room wearing just a towel. At first, I told them where to stick their idea, but in the end, just to shut them up, I did it, begrudgingly. Even though I had lost a considerable amount of weight since high school, I wasn't confident appearing with my shirt off in front of people, let alone just wearing a towel. There was a point there when the guys were heckling me, where I had flashbacks to my high school bullying days.

I did it, and I think I beat Seph in the looking embarrassed department, as when I did it Thys, the little Italian bastard, whipped my towel off, giving himself, Nivek, and—worst of all—Seph, a millisecond glimpse of my entire naked body. I think, when I had made it through the living room, with my hands hiding all I could, I hid in my room for the rest of the night, embarrassed as hell and hating Thys and Nivek.

The softest of raps on my purple, bedroom door had told me who it was, Seph always knocked, unlike the other two. I heard her but chose to ignore her by quickly switching on my Walkman and blaring SAHB'S, Sensational Alex Harvey Band, Boston Tea Party into my eardrums and shutting my eyes. I was lying on my bed in the darkness of my room; the only light coming in was through the window. As I faced the door, I noticed that the blackness that I saw through my closed eyelids shifted a shade lighter. The shadow, if you will, of light passed and all was black again.

At the time, I thought Seph had peered in and shut the door again, but she hadn't. I felt the mattress go down as she sat on the side of the bed. Doing my best to fake sleep, I felt a touch that was like electricity as fingers brushed my hair and gently stroked the side of my face—the physical connection with Seph that I had longed for from the moment I met her. The soft, tender touch traced my jawline and lightly skipped over my lips. I still faked sleep, not wanting to disturb this unexpected term of affection, but still wanting to reciprocate. I felt the beginnings of a sneeze coming, and try as I might, I could not stifle it. I wrinkled and crinkled my nose, but to my dismay, it happened. As soon as I entered the beginning stages, I felt the weight leave my bed and opened my eyes in time to see; not Seph, but Nivek leave my bedroom!

I was left with a cocktail of emotions. The warm ecstatic glow of happiness that I had felt when I had thought it was Seph was the flagrant, flamboyant liquid, and the stone-cold shock of the realisation that it was, in fact, Nivek, stabbed like the miniature umbrella, an unwanted intruder. I sat for hours, not hearing my SAHB songs, but wondering what to do or say about the incident. The only decision I came to was to pretend it never happened. As far as I know, he thought I hadn't seen him, so I was happy with that. I will admit to giving him the cold shoulder for the following few days, but that was because I didn't know what to say to him. He acted the same, friendly as normal.

In a way, my attack made me momentarily forget this encounter.

For as long as I knew him, he never showed any other signs of homosexuality, but, like Seph would often catch me, I would often catch Nivek staring at me with his pale ghost-like face. I couldn't imagine how traumatic it was for him, being attracted, well that's if it was an attraction, to a man who wasn't the same sexuality as he. And to think, how torn-up I was when Seph came back from a shift at The Drum and announced that she had met a bloke.

The announcement hit harder than any punch or kick that my assailants in the park had thrown twelve months previously. She came into the house interrupting the conversation we three stooges had been having, smiling from ear to ear. We all looked at her in surprise, as her usual demeanour when she arrived home from work was one of complete exhaustion. She would come, drop her bag on the floor, take off her coat and throw it in the direction of the coat cupboard, and crash in the nearest armchair and simply demand, "Tea!" Or on particularly bad nights, "Beer!"

But not this night; she came in, perched on the side of the settee and smiled, and asked us what we were talking about. Obviously, we knew something was up by the way she was beaming like a Cheshire cat. I asked her why she was so happy, had she been given a pay rise etc.... She just acted coy and said she had just had a good shift. I left it. However, Thys, ever the persistent one, wouldn't have it, so he pestered her until she gave in and told us.

"Umm... errr... I've sort of met someone..."

My blood ran cold as I tried my best not to let my face display my inner feelings.

"Yeah, this guy came in tonight, and we got talking... He's really sweet, not like the other wankers and old perverts that you get in there ..."

Nivek was the only one who appeared genuinely pleased for her. I tried my best and Thys, now he knew why she was happy, was more interested in the TV than Seph.

"So what's he like then?" Nivek asked, sitting forward, staring at Seph with excited eyes. He was becoming campier every day.

Seph smirked. "Well, to be honest, he's not the kind I'd usually fancy, but there's just something about him. We just got on really well, and he was so sweet and very complimentary."

My heart shattered into a million pieces, but I managed to prevent the segments from spilling out and onto the settee.

Nivek smiled his black-lipped smile. "What does he look like?"

"He's got short dirty-blonde hair and a couple of piercings looks like a slightly rugged version of Jude Law."

"Ah right," Nivek said thinking for a second, "So what sort of things is he into?"

Seph looked slightly embarrassed. "Well, this is where the opposites attract thing comes into it. He's into all that R'n'B shit and hip-hop."

Nivek, myself, and even Thys, who turned away from the TV when he heard that, looked at her with pained expressions on our faces.

"It's only music, for Christ's sake!" Seph said harshly, "If you're going to discriminate just because someone likes a different genre of music from you then you're no better than a bunch of fucking Chavs!"

"So is that what he is?" Thys dared to ask.

Seph looked hurt. "No, he isn't, well maybe just a little."

"So," I said, "What this bloke's name?"

"Stuart. We're going to the cinema tomorrow night."

"Oh, this should be good," Thys began, "What film?"

Seph flushed red, "You've Got Mail"

A chorus of astonished 'No's' erupted around the room. Seph was a horror film fanatic and had most of the Japanese horror flicks on video before they were made fashionable.

Over-dramatizing, I jumped up and tried my best to look disgusted, "You've Got Mail? I'm sorry, but I cannot stay in the same room as someone who is prepared to not only sit through but also pay to sit through a romantic comedy starring Meg Ryan and Tom Hanks. I'm going to bed!" I walked towards the stairs, listening to them all laughing.

"Yeah, but I'm not paying for it, and I might get a shag out of it!" Seph called half-joking. Thys and Nivek laughed, as did I, but that line alone dug itself into my chest and picked up all the pieces of my heart and pulverized them with an imaginary steak mallet. As I climbed the stairs, I heard her mention something about 'doggy-style' and upon hearing that; the remnants of my mashed-up heart were put into a food blender at high speed. I cried myself to sleep that night.

I was stupid really. Did I honestly expect Seph to stay single forever? Yes! She should've become celibate and become a nun until the day I plucked up enough courage to confess my feelings.

And seeing as I had never had the courage to tell her my feelings, how was she supposed to know that I secretly worshipped the ground she walked upon? And that the fact that this was the first boyfriend she was going to have since I knew her was going to put me through sheer agony whenever I saw them together? At that point, I got to the stage where I considered either moving out or living back with my parents in my shitty village or moving out and trying to hook up somewhere else to live. Either way, I couldn't bear to be around the place when I found out she'd met someone.

Their first date went excellently, apparently. He was a real gentleman. Whenever she was due to go on a date with him, I volunteered for overtime at work and stopped on with the night fillers in the supermarket. I didn't like doing that, as it meant having to walk across town at midnight, and ever since the attack, I was paranoid. I would walk hurriedly along the deserted High Street with my hand in my pocket, clutching the Stanley knife I used at work.

So yeah, I managed to avoid him for about four weeks in total. I started locking my bedroom door so I could pretend to be out when Seph made attempts at trying to introduce him to me. I kept an emergency supply of food for when he came round unexpectedly, and worst of all, I kept an empty, three-litre bottle, in case I needed the toilet. I didn't even see him until the fourth week! Nivek and Thys quizzed me on why I went out of my way to avoid Seph and Stuart, but I put it down to circumstances. But I knew that, as much as I tried, I wouldn't be able to avoid him or them forever and I, eventually, saw him accidentally.

It was a Saturday night, and everyone was supposed to be at the free music festival in Christchurch Park. I made some excuse that I couldn't go and stayed in. I came out of my room to go downstairs to get a drink, but as I descended, I saw that the living room light was on and I could hear the TV was playing some dodgy comedy programme. I crept down silently and peered at the settee. From where I was standing, I could see the back of Seph's head obscuring Stuart's face. They were kissing. Just as I was about to turn around and creep slowly back up the stairs, a tremendous burst of laughter came from the television, and I saw Seph turn her head to look at the TV. I got a full shot of Stuart's face. It was the man who had attacked me in the park!

After failing to give the police a decent enough description, I only bloody recognised him. I was terrified; I stumbled as I ran up the stairs and slammed my door against their childish laughter. I had a predicament.

CHAPTER FOUR

I had a predicament. I sat for a while in my bedroom, frightened, my heart thudding in my chest. The laughing downstairs made me feel sick. I had visions of Seph making me come down and introducing me to my attacker. What would I say? Surely he would recognise me. I put my headphones on to drown out their laughter while I thought of something to do. Half of me wanted to call the police, but the other half wanted to go downstairs and confront him. But what if I did? Would he deny it? Would he turn nasty? Knowing that he had a temper on him made me even more determined to get him away from Seph.

I stood up and crossed my room with the intention of picking up my mobile phone and calling the police. But as my hand reached out to pick up my phone, I noticed the Stanley knife I used for work sitting next to it. For some reason, another part of me, hidden up until then, picked up the knife instead. It was only when I had the knife in my hand that I realised there was another option. For the first time in my life, I wanted revenge!

I felt as though I was in a trance, even though I knew exactly what I was going to do. I put a pair of jeans on and the nearest jumper I could find. I opened my bedroom door a crack so that I could hear the muffled murmur of voices. I think I must have sat on the floor for about an hour, hour and a half before I heard them at the front door. I tried to ignore all the sickening lovey-dovey shit they were saying and waited for Stuart to finally leave. I heard Seph say 'goodbye' for the umpteenth time and close the front door. As soon as she'd done this, I shut and locked my own and opened my window. I climbed out of my window and carefully lowered myself onto the roof of the kitchen extension. I walked across the roof and lowered myself again onto a big green wheelie bin. I remember grazing my back on the edge of the roof and swearing. Hoping that Seph wouldn't hear me, I jogged up the side of the house and looked in both directions. I could see him walking slowly, head down, about fifty yards away from me.

I began to follow him, walking quickly at first but then slowing so that he wouldn't notice me. I had the knife in my pocket, even though I never intended to use it on him. It was just for my own protection. As he continued on and into the town centre, his mobile rang and I heard his half of the conversation. From what I could make out, he was talking about Seph. What I heard him say went roughly like this:

"Alright mate? Nah I'm going to go McDonald's way... Yeah, I just been round that barmaid's... Huh? Oh, Seph, what? Yeah, I know it's a pretty stupid name, short for Parsippany or something.... Nah man, she hasn't... Sure I've had a grope or two, but she hasn't let me fuck her yet..."

The bastard continued to spit out obscenities about Seph, making me hate him even more. Eventually, after I had to endure what he wanted to do to Seph, in far too much detail, he finished his phone conversation and hung up. We went up the empty High Street—all the shops were protected by their metal roller shutters. There were a few drunken revellers cheering and whooping at nothing obvious, but High Street was mostly quiet. Stuart took a right turn that leads up past McDonald's. The road was a lot less lit, and I became scared of what I was doing. I was about to turn around and go home, wimping out on my task, when Stuart suddenly spun around on his heels and faced me. "Why are you following...?" He began, but then a look of recognition made his eyes go wide, and a cruel smile appeared on his face. "Oh my god, it's you!" he said almost laughing.

I stood rooted to the spot, frozen in fear. He frowned, a look of amusement still on his face. "So, you want a repeat of what you got last year, or are you going to fuck off?" I was amazed he gave me the option. I was about to turn around and count my lucky stars when I found the courage to speak to him.

"I want you to leave Seph alone." He looked surprised at the sound of her name.

"How do you know her?" I began to answer but he guessed before I had a chance to. "You're one of her flatmates!" He laughed at the realisation. "Fucking hell!"

I nodded. "Leave her alone." Stuart's face turned from that of amusement to anger, "Fuck you. I'm not leaving her alone. You're the one who's going to leave her alone. I'm going to fuck her senseless. Move out, or I'll fucking cripple you!" I was trembling inside, I thought that sooner or later I would give in and he would either pulverise me or I would run away. Stuart started to turn, and as he did, he said, "Hey, as soon as I've finished with the fat cunt, you can have a go, call it an apology for the beating like."

That did it for me, I threw myself at him. I pushed him as hard as I could and watched as he spun around and attempted to hit me. Luckily, he lost his balance and missed me. I took this opportunity to throw my first-ever punch. My right fist connected with his face, and I was amazed to actually see his nose pour with blood. I stepped back as he held a hand up to his nose and stared in bewilderment at the blood.

"You bastard." He said and lunged at me. He grabbed hold of me and put me in a headlock and began to squeeze my neck. Colours started to erupt in front of my eyes as he began to choke me, my face pressed up against his stomach. My hot, sweaty face touched his cold clammy skin as his shirt had rucked up in our struggle. Try as I did to get hold of him, I just couldn't get him off me. As a last resort, I pulled the Stanley knife out of my pocket, withdrew the blade, and ran it across his bare stomach. He immediately released me and screamed in pain and fell away, clutching his cut belly. I stood, shocked at what I had done. Stuart looked at me, equally shocked. His face was beginning to pale as the blood that ran from his wound soaked his shirt and the front of his trousers.

"You fucker!" he said with frightened eyes.

I snapped out of my zombie-like state, dropping the knife onto the cold, littered concrete floor. I moved toward Stuart, just as scared as he. He backed away from me until the wall stopped him. I didn't know what to do. I know I should have helped him, but I still hated the bastard for what he had done to me and what he had said about Seph. I pulled off my jumper and folded it up with the idea of using it to press against Stuart's wound. When I got close to him, he freaked out and started flailing his arms about to fight me off. I could see that he was losing too much blood; he was as white as a ghost.

He staggered away from me, fumbling in his pocket as he went. He removed his mobile phone and dialled a number and shakily held the phone up to his ear. Panicking, I quickly knocked the phone out of his hand and pushed him down onto a window-ledge on the McDonald's beside us. "Stay still, I'm not going to hurt you. I'm ringing an ambulance for you." I tried to sound as reassuring as I could as I picked up his mobile phone. I was amazed at how little blood I had got on me. I dialled triple nine and told Stuart to tell them where he was.

He screamed down the phone to the operator. He informed them that he had been stabbed and of his whereabouts. I pocketed the phone and put my jumper back on. Stealing one last look at him slouched on the bench, the dark-patch on his stomach getting wider and wider, I should have felt sorry for him. But I didn't. I was happy. He deserved some of his own medicine. How many people had he and his mate beaten and mugged in the past? Surely, this would put him off. This was a good thing. A new wave of terror befell him as I crouched down and picked up my knife.

Looming over him, I smiled, "That was for Seph. This is for me." I swiftly ran the blade across his throat and walked away; his gurgling died out the further away I got.

As I walked slowly back to the house, I was amazed at what I had done. The thing that scared me was that I knew exactly what I was doing; I was totally in control of my thoughts. I had wanted revenge, and I had got it. I had murdered somebody. Surprisingly, I was abnormally calm. I would panic at the slightest of things, but after the murder, I coped just fine.

A million thoughts were racing through my head, the main one being that it was only a matter of time before I was arrested and locked away. But as I thought of the negative things, another part of me kept chirruping up with helpful optimistic points. How could the police connect it to me if I never owned up to Stuart being one of the attackers who jumped me last year? I checked myself over as I walked, I had almost no blood on me whatsoever, and besides, the police wouldn't have had any fingerprints or shit like that off me, as until then, I had never been in trouble. The only people that had been about were pissed out of their puny brains and they were long gone when we had our confrontation. Unless the police did a house to house D.N.A test throughout the whole town and the surrounding suburbs, there was no way I could be caught!

    I seemed to take hardly any time getting home. I felt exhilarated, my heart was beating fast, and I felt alert and capable of doing anything. I realised what it was, the buzz of killing. I went back to my room the same way I came out of it, up onto the wheelie bin and onto the kitchen roof. It took hardly any effort at all.

    When I was in my bedroom, I switched the light on and stood in front of the full-length mirror in my wardrobe. I checked my clothing for blood stains and there were none. It must have been due to the fact that my head was near where I cut him. I noticed a bit of blood in my hair, adding to the black and blonde streaks. After removing my clothes and putting them in my laundry basket, I changed into a T-shirt and jean cut-offs and went downstairs with the intention of using the shower.

I was surprised to see that Seph was still down there. She was curled up on the settee in pyjama bottoms and a vest top. She even looked beautiful asleep. I smirked at the position she was in. She was on her side, knees up towards her chest, resting her head on hands that were pressed together as if in prayer. Every now and then, her eyelids would flicker and her delicate lips would part as she exhaled. Forgetting why I had gone downstairs, I wanted to stand there for hours. Noticing that it was a bit chilly in the room, I hauled her coat—which lay in its usual resting place—over the back of an armchair, and as gently as I could, covered her with it. I wasn't gentle enough; she stirred, blinked a few times, and smiled groggily up at me.

"Hey." I returned her 'hey' with a 'Yo'. She yawned a few times and sat up. "What you doing up so late?"

"I need a shower. I crashed when I got back from work and only woke up a while ago." I lied.

"Oh God," Seph said, sitting forward, putting her face in her hands, her red hair falling over her naked shoulders.

"Yes," I said, answering my nickname. She looked up apologetically at me. "I know you caught us earlier. I'm sorry. We weren't laughing at you. We were laughing because we'd been caught."

I shrugged, "Hey don't worry about it, just wish it could've been me." Seph went wide-eyed at precisely the same time as I groaned and realised what I had said. "No, I don't mean kissing you..."

Seph gasped, "Kissing Stuart!?"

I laughed, "No! I meant I wish it could've been me on the sofa snogging someone!" I praised myself for my quick thinking.

Seph pouted. "Oh, you'll find someone soon." Then with a burst of girlish excitement, "Hey, we'll be able to go on double dates!"

"Is it going that well?" I asked her, sitting myself opposite.

She frowned. "What do you mean?"

"I mean, do you think you'll still be with him when I'm about fifty?"

"Fifty?"

"Yeah, because that's how old I'll be when I finally meet someone," Seph smirked and rolled her eyes. Then she looked at my hair. My blood ran cold, I could feel it crystallising in my veins until she spoke.

"Hey, love the red, it's really cool. How long you had that in for?" Phew!

"Oh... umm... I put some of that wash-in wash-out stuff in earlier, just to see what it looked like before I do it permanently. It's now going to be washed out."

As I made for the bathroom, Seph called out, "Night, don't forget to clean the pubes out of the plughole!"

I think I showered about three times just to make sure. I had taken the Stanley knife out of my jeans upstairs and washed and disinfected it in the bathroom sink. I sat on the toilet-seat inspecting Stuart's mobile phone. I was quite surprised that it was the same make as mine, one of those Nokias that you could change the fascias of. You can find out a lot about somebody through their mobile phone. What things interest them. What things they find funny. What music they like. Stuart's was how a stereotypical hooligan's phone should be, filled with pictures of either Page-Three girls, or football emblems.

I scanned the pictures, each one flitting in front of my eyes tediously. Two pictures that stood out for me were one of his friends, who helped in my attack. His name was Jez, I kept that in mind for future reference, and the other picture was one of me lying unconscious on the ground at the Second World War monument in Christchurch Park!

I read through all of his saved text messages, though there was nothing of interest. I pocketed it and went to bed and went to sleep, slightly concerned about what dreams might follow.

CHAPTER FIVE

Well, the dreams that followed weren't of any importance, just one of being at a SAHB concert and The Man singing to me. The only thing that seemed a bit odd, but didn't occur to me at the time, was that whilst he was on stage, he was staring straight at me and he had a mobile phone that looked identical to Stuart's. In my imagination, maybe that was some subliminal message, but try as I might, I can't figure out what.

The morning after I committed my first murder, I remember waking up to the sound of tears being wept. Seph's room was next door to mine, and I could hear her quite clearly. As soon as I stirred, I saw my door open and Nivek walked in, wearing a solemn expression on his pale face. He sat down on my bed, and before he had a chance to speak, I beat him to it.

"Niv mate, what's the matter with Seph?"

He rubbed a hand over his face, "You're not going to believe this..."

"What?"

"Stuart, Seph's boyfriend, has been murdered!" He said in half disbelief.

I was speechless, "What? How?"

"Apparently, he was found outside McDonald's. He'd been stabbed and had his phone stolen. His best mate Jez rang Seph this morning, and I've just read about it in the paper. It's all over the front page and on the local news."

"Jesus. I don't believe it! I never even met the guy! Oh man." I tried my best to be shocked, and I think I convinced Nivek. He sat down on my bed beside me, crossed his legs, and just stared at the wall with a blank expression. We were all pretty young, and neither of us had had to deal with death before. I didn't want to comfort him physically because I suspected him of having some carnal inclinations towards me, so I just acted the same as he did until things moved on.

Seph stayed in her room for several days. We guys took it in turns to take her food and water, of which the food was discarded. You can't imagine just how guilty I felt. Not for killing that bastard, but for causing Seph so much pain. I hated hearing her sobs through my bedroom wall. But she didn't really know him! She only loved the man who he pretended to be, just to get her into bed. He would never have worshipped her the way I did and still do.

Several times, I found myself standing outside her bedroom, staring and the tattered Marillion poster on the door, Stuart's mobile phone in my hand, so tempted to show her what he was really like. But no, I didn't. For one, it'd mean I'd be jailed, but I also didn't want to cause her any more pain, even if it was a different kind. Which is easier, to love somebody who's dead, or hate somebody who's dead? If you were to love somebody who's dead, you would be filled with regrets, that you didn't have a chance to say 'goodbye', thoughts of what it would be like if they were still alive. But if you hate someone who's dead, wouldn't you be filled with resentment and frustrated that you never had a chance to tell them you hated them, never had a chance for revenge?

Seph finally came out of her room a week later, looking exhausted and broken.

As for the murder of Stuart, after three weeks of door to door inquiries throughout the town, much to my surprise, the police charged somebody for it.

Apparently, Stuart and his mate, Jez, were in trouble with a big nasty gang of drug users and dealers in town who frequented the park. When Jez had confessed this to the police, the police raided the known accommodation of the alleged gang, and they found one of Stuart's bloodied trainers at the bottom of a bin outside their house. They arrested the gang leader, a man who went by the name of Skinner. A few of the other gang members were arrested and given a few months' sentence. They all had their pictures in the paper. Proper rough-looking thugs of mixed ethnicity.

According to the newspaper article that came out the day after Stuart was murdered, he was found wearing only one trainer. I was really baffled by that. Then a terrifying thought occurred to me. What if Stuart had been followed? Someone else apart from me? My sensible, rational side argued that surely, if this was true, then the gang would have told the police that I did the dastardly deed. So I temporarily put the thought out of my head and marvelled at how lucky I was.

So eventually, life got back to normal. As Seph had missed so much work, she was working every hour they could give her so she could afford her part of the rent. She never mentioned Stuart's name until she found out about the rumour in the paper about him being involved with drug users. She told me that she didn't believe it.

Just when things had died down about Stuart's murder, Nivek gave us all something else to talk about. He came out of the proverbial closet. Seph, Thys, and I were chilling in front of the telly when Nivek came home with a stranger in tow. The other guy was a bit shorter and plumper than Niv wore glasses and had a wicked goatee. We three mumbled a 'Hello' to the new guy and looked at Niv expectantly as if to say 'Well, Niv mate, aren't you going to introduce us?' But Niv just looked at us sheepishly, and then spun round to face the newbie. He grabbed him by the back of the neck and pulled his face towards him and planted a very passionate black-lipped kiss upon his lips. The kiss lasted five seconds, and from where I was seated, I could see a great deal of tongue usage. I had strong inklings of Nivek's sexuality, but I still sat mouth agape.

Thys screamed out "Whoa!" and Seph copied me. Nivek hadn't just pushed the closet door open a crack, just to see what it was like outside, he'd kicked the fucker off the hinges and leapt out into the Kingdom of Gay. When the kiss was kissed, Niv turned to us all questioningly. Thys sat, shaking his head, his face recoiling in horror.

Seph broke the silence; she smiled and jumped up excitedly. "Oh, excellent! Niv, mate, you never said you were gay, that's brilliant!" She hugged him and the new guy, who appeared to be embarrassed. I thought I'd better say something, but the only thing I could think of was, 'Yeah that's cool. Gay's the new straight!' What a fucking stupid thing to say!

Nivek seemed to relax a bit, but it wasn't long before all of our faces were on Thys. His own still held the expression of shock. Nivek addressed Thys. "Thys, you're not my type. I don't like my men tanned, so fuck off!"

Thys let out a sigh of relief. "Oh thank God for that! I thought I was going to have to move out"

"Anyway, this is my…" Nivek seemed to have difficulty saying the word, "boyfriend, Colin." I couldn't help myself, I burst into laughter.

"Kevin and Colin you even sound like a gay couple!" Niv shot me a cold glance, and Colin was the one who spoke. I was surprised to find out he had a Scottish accent.

"Well, that's what we are."

"Yeah," Niv added, "and it's not Kevin, and you bloody well know that!"

I managed to chew back the laughter that still wanted to erupt from me until Colin spoke again. "If it's any consolation, to try and make my name sound less shit, I spell it K-O-L-'-N." The tiniest of sniggers came from me and was greeted by stony looks from Seph and the two gays. Thys did the laughing for me, and Seph apologised on his behalf. After an hour of being hit by Seph and getting all the gay-related innuendoes out that Thys and I could think of, we accepted the fact. The conversation progressed and Kol'n turned out to be a really nice bloke and hilariously funny too. We soon welcomed him into the bosom of our family, and he became a regular member of the household.

One thing that had been nagging at me since I started was my job at the time, working in the supermarket. With the brain-dead harpies and the mindless fuckwits. My boss was a short, fat little bastard by the name of John Goodchild. He was about five-foot-four and ginger and smelled constantly—a putrid concoction of sweat, feet, and garlic. I hardly ever saw him anyway, which was good, it was mostly the assistant manager or one of the supervisors that hung around. I usually minded my own business, coming into work doing whatever chores Goodchild, the assistant manager or the three supervisors set me to perform. My usual day would consist of loading up cages in the warehouse for the women who weren't on checkout to put on the shop floor. If—which was mostly the case—the women struggled with the number of cages, then I would be summoned to go out and help them. I'd hate to do this as what it'd usually involve is me teaming up with one of the girls and assisting her in putting out the products. Which always meant that I'd put it all out, whilst the woman would stand and talk to one of the other workers, or some customer who was a relative. Every now and then, whoever I was working with would look up at me and mutter something to the person they were with. Laughter would follow. To be fair, most of the people weren't all that bad, they'd not go out of their way to speak to me, and that was fine.

The worst person was Nivek's mother, the bitch, or to use her birth name, Lorraine. Skinny, blonde, and severely burnt out, she looked like someone had left her in the bath too long, wrinkled like a prune and covered with a really bad fake tan. She was a chain smoker and had teeth like ancient, roadside, moss-covered milestones. When she laughed, it sounded like a fusion of water going down a plughole and someone with severe emphysema. Laden in gold jewellery and plastered in several layers of cheap cosmetics, she looked a picture.

She was my nemesis at work. As soon as she and Nivek's dad found out about his homosexuality, they completely disowned him. They didn't have anything to do with him in the first place really. They didn't like that he wasn't like them. It wasn't just his image, it was everything. He had intellect, desired better things for himself, had ambition, wanted to go out there and see the world, in fact, he and Kol'n started to save up so they could do the stereotypical student-thing and take a year out of college and backpack across Europe. There were a few moments where I was tempted to invite myself into their venture, but the thought of not being in the same country as Seph alarmed me.

But yeah, Nivek's parents disowned him. It was their loss. When they had found out about him being gay, the jibes at work from Lorraine increased, and she would say harsh stuff at me with hatred in her eyes. For some reason, she thought I was gay. I don't know why maybe it was because I was single. Even though she said that sort of stuff before Nivek came out, when she said it, it was because he was a Goth and wore make-up, not because they actually knew he was gay, and somehow, that wasn't as bad as them hating the real thing.

CHAPTER SIX

It was after a blissful day at work when I came home and, as soon as I walked exhaustedly through the door, Seph approached me with a newspaper. I immediately thought it was something to do with Stuart's murder. You tend to get a bit paranoid when you've murdered someone, trust me. I frowned at her and sat on the arm of a chair.

Taking the paper when she offered it to me, I said, "What's this?" The first thing I saw when I looked at the paper was an article with a photo of Stuart's mate, Jez, with the headline: 'THUG GOES FREE DUE TO TERRIFIED WITNESSES!'

I saw that he was still up to his old games. I knew that wasn't what Seph wanted me to look at. I lowered my eyes and saw a circled advert. Upon reading it, I saw that it was advertising a school reunion. A reunion of school leavers from my school in the year I left. "It's a bit soon, isn't it?"

Seph nodded. "I think you should go!"

I laughed and said, "No way, I hated that school. They were all bastards there!"

"Oh come on, there must be someone who you'd like to meet up with?" Seph said, smiling when she saw the smile that appeared on my face.

"Well, there's a couple of mates who I've lost touch with and... err... someone else too."

Seph's eyes lit up, "A girl? Wooooooooooooooooooo," Actually I think there should have been a few more O's there. "You never told me about your high school sweetheart." She crashed down on the settee. "Come on. Tell all."

I rolled my eyes. "Oh bollocks. It's nothing. When I was at school, I had a major crush on this girl..."

"None of 'this girl' malarkey, I want a name!"

I sighed, "Okay. Her name was Katie Dearsley, we went to the same Primary school and High school, and I had a major crush on her all the way through, for at least ten years!"

Seph grinned. "Aww. So did you ever....?"

I shook my head. "I never even spoke to her; no, actually that's a lie. I spoke to her once in the last year of Primary school. We were doing art one afternoon and there were some workmen in the classroom so all the tables had been jiggled about. I had to sit at the same table as her. I remember I was drawing a picture of a giant destroying a building. You see, we had to draw a picture inspired by one of the books we'd been reading that term. I'd read Roald Dahl's BFG, and I dropped my tin of colouring pencils on the floor, and she helped me pick them up. She looked at my picture and said that she 'liked it and that it was really, really cool.' I said, 'thank you,' and she gave me the sweetest smile I'd ever seen."

Seph said something that was so high-pitched, only dogs would have been able to hear it. Just some indecipherable girl-squeal. I laughed, feeling my cheeks flush. "That's sooo sweet!" Seph said beaming. "You must go to this reunion! It's fate's way of telling you that you have another chance to pull the woman of your dreams!" Little did she know, the 'woman of my dreams' was sitting there before me.

"No, I can't. There's no saying she'll be there anyhow." Seph tutted and grabbed the article.

After a few seconds, she piped up again. "Tell you what. It's in a pub the other side of town, so I'll come with you and we can just have a drink and see if she's there. Don't worry, I won't make you do anything you don't want to, I promise. And, before you think it, I won't go up to her and tell her you have an undying love for her. Deal?"

How could I resist going out alone with Seph? As traumatic as I thought it may be, I couldn't miss the opportunity to be alone with the real woman of my dreams. "Ok, but not a word of this to Marilyn Manson and Mussolini?" They were some of my pet names for Thys and Niv.

"Deal!" Seph squeaked and lunged forward and stretched out her hand. Fucking hell, I thought. I shook her hand. I wish she'd realised that even the merest of physical contact drove me insane.

And so came the night of the school reunion. The pub, a shitty little number that went by the commonly used name, The Golden Lion, was dingy and drab. Seph had advised me on what to wear; she said I shouldn't appear to be too 'alternative', but I could still be a little rough around the edges. Whatever the fuck that meant. After painstakingly trying on numerous T-shirt, shirt, and trouser combinations, we finally agreed on baggy blue jeans, a close-fitting black T-shirt and, I don't know where the hell she found it, a floral shirt embroidered with red and pink flowers. I thought it a tad feminine, but Seph said it was sexy. I selected a pink lip ring and all was ready.

I spent about an hour waiting for Seph to get ready, and when she came into the living room, I was completely lost for words. She looked more beautiful than I thought was possible. She wore knee-high black boots over fishnets and a knee-length wrap-around dress that was black with zillions of little white dots on it. Her beautiful red hair cascaded over the low-cut back. She wore make–up, despite the fact that she didn't need it, but it was minimal, black eyeliner and red glossy lipstick. God, how I longed to kiss those lips!

So yeah, back to the pub. It was what you'd call a 'local' pub. As soon as we went in there, everyone looked at us. To be fair, there weren't that many patrons in there at the time, as it was early—just a couple of old men. But they visibly perved over Seph as she glided towards the bar, looking like a movie star, and ordered two pints of Kronenbourg. Not exactly Hollywood, but that's what I liked about her.

I wondered why the person who had organised this 'event' had chosen such a shitty meeting place. I figured that it had to be their local. Doing a quick scan of the place, I saw no one that appeared to be of my age. Seph thrust a cold pint into my hand and we went and found a table in a dark corner in view of the main door, so we could see if anyone came in.

We sat and chatted about childish things, college, future goals, and music, for around an hour and a half. By the time the next punter came in, we were quite pissed, and when Seph nudged me, asking if the customer looked familiar, I sobered up immediately. He didn't see me, but I saw him and recognised him. Sure it hadn't been a drastic amount of years since I left High, but I'd changed a bit. But He looked the same. Ross Atkins. I watched uncomfortably as he strode casually up to the bar and ordered. Atkins stood at about six feet; he'd grown a bit since school. He still had the stupid short, black spiky hair that he had. He looked like the offspring of Aerosmith's frontman, Steve Tyler; he had a huge wide mouth and tiny evil little eyes. He was still a skinny bastard too. In the time it took him to walk to the bar, a whole five years of torment flashed back at me. Meeting him not long after I first started High on the playground. There I was, in my mind's eye, I stood against a wall with my geeky friend, David, eating, because I was forever on a diet, a crispbread. All of a sudden, Atkins and a couple of his mates surrounded us; their main attention was on me.

"What's your name?"

Looking at my shiny black shoes. "Robert Goddard."

Eyeing me up and down, "Why are you eating that?"

"Because I'm on a diet," I mumbled incoherently.

"What did you say?" said Atkins, looking so stony at me.

A little bit louder, "Because I'm on a diet." A few sniggers from his mates.

Then Atkins spoke again, "Well your diet doesn't seem to be working, does it?" I remained silent. "It can't be working because you're a fat bastard." His mates laughed at him. I looked towards David, but he was pretending not to notice. "Did you hear what I said?" Atkins shouted. I returned his shout with a nod. "You're a fat bastard aren't you?"

I said nothing.

"Aren't you?!"

I reluctantly nodded my head. Atkins loomed over me and pushed me up against the wall, forcing me to look him in the face. "Say it! Shout out 'I'm a fat bastard' now, or else!" I shook my head, tears welling up in my eyes. He grabbed hold of my jumper. "Say it!"

I saw my eleven-year-old self in the playground up against the wall and heard myself shout, "I'm a fat bastard," as the whole playground erupted into uncontrollable laughter.

Another time that felt its need to flashback was when I was standing outside the science lab waiting for the lesson to start with all the other kids. Atkins and his mates shared the same lesson with me, and I shuddered inwardly as they approached. Atkins came straight up to me and pushed me up against some metal lockers. He put both hands on my chest and squeezed the excess fat there and grinned.

"Goddard's got tits!" He felt the need to share with everyone. He turned back to me, "Do you not like me?" What sort of fucking question was that? Did he honestly expect me to say, "Yes, of course, I like you?" As I was scared shitless of him, that's exactly what I did say. We looked towards the corridor as we heard the distant whistling of the approaching science teacher. Letting go of me he grabbed my crotch and walked off.

The other such occasions during my several second flashbacks were similar variations of those two.

Back to reality.

As he accepted his bottle of Budweiser from the barman, he too scanned the pub for old schoolmates. My heart was beating like a drum, Seph had noticed that I'd gone whiter than a sheet, but being the smart girl, that she was kept quiet until Atkins, much to my relief simply eyed Seph up and walked off to another table on the opposite side of the pub and sat down. I wouldn't explain to Seph why I had reacted that way when Atkins came in. I simply told her I didn't want to discuss it, and that I would tell her at a later date. She told me that if he took the piss out of me at school she would go over there and 'kick the fucker's head in'. I loved her for saying that.

We soon changed the subject when a few other people came in whom I recognised. A couple of men, who I remembered to be in my art class, whose surnames I forgot, but first names were Paul and Daniel. I didn't have that many friends at school, and I wasn't really expecting any of them to turn up. Paul and Daniel just simply nodded a greeting, eyed up Seph, and went to find a seat. And so the night drew on.

We had several drinks, and nature finally took its course and I needed the toilet. Finding myself a bit wobbly, I staggered to the toilets in a desperate battle against my drunken legs, so that I might empty five pints of Kronenbourg from my bladder. I was typically drunk, bursting into the lavatory, stumbling into the nearest available cubicle, slamming the door shut, and leaning against the door. Jesus, I remember it being the longest piss that had ever been pissed from my pisser. A couple of times I almost drifted off to sleep leaning against that door.

    I finally let myself out of the cubicle and went over to the sinks trying my best to avoid walking into the other man who was there. As I turned the cold tap on, I heard an oh so familiar voice, that had earlier that evening featured in a number of flashbacks, say, "Goddard!!!!" I immediately sobered up once I looked up into the mirror in front of the sink to see Atkins beside me, his wide mouth exaggerating the grin he had on his face.

CHAPTER SEVEN

Before I tell you what happened next, I want to tell you just how much I hated Ross Atkins. You had a brief glimpse at how he used to treat me in High School, and I will spare you the endless other ordeals he put me through. But my resentment for him should have ended the day I left school; I went to a different college than him and had not seen him from the last day of school until that day in The Golden Lion.

Maybe I was right to hold a grudge against him for the years of torment I endured. My hatred got so bad in my first year of Art College, that when we were given a new project on the topic of Emotions, I immediately chose Hate. We had to choose three different emotions, and mine weren't all negative. But Hate developed into a sort of revenge tactic for me. I did a series of six pieces. Each one depicted something that I hated. The first piece was a sculpture of a head and shoulders done using clay. I sculpted a sneering face covered in a few scars and wearing a baseball cap. I made some gold jewellery from looped-wire painted gold. Basically, it was the upper torso of a chav, but the word 'chav' had not been in use then.

My second piece was a sketching of a deserted high street that had all its bins overturned and litter everywhere. Rotten vegetables, empty take away cartons, half-eaten junk food, nappies, anything I could think of that I've seen discarded in the streets of my town.

The third piece was done in pastel, and I'll admit, pretty sick. On A0 black paper done in chalks, it showed a black man kneeling on the ground, his hands held up before his face to protect him and to plead with the looming figure of a Ku Klux Klan member standing above him with a burning torch held aloft.

The fourth piece was a bit of a laugh really. I did a painted portrait of three comedians, famous for their racist humour in the pre-eighties.

The fifth was a painting of a typical scenario from a football game. A guy skidding to tackle the occupier of the ball.

The sixth and the centrepiece was a virtually life-sized pastel on black paper of a young man hanging from a noose around his neck. Eyes bulging face purplish, tongue lolling out. He was intentionally wearing my High School uniform. It was Ross Atkins hanging. Obviously, I never actually admitted to anyone that it was he. I told everyone that it stood for my hatred of suicide. I remember Nivek, who was then in the same class as me, looking in amazement at my exhibition when I revealed it at the end of the Hate project. I'm sad to say I don't recall much of Niv's work from that project; the only thing I remember was that one of the emotions that he chose was also Hate, and he did a picture of an aborted foetus, which still haunts me to this day.

The other two emotions I chose were Love and Happiness. See not all doom and gloom. For Love, I did a few obligatory family portraits, a life-sized Alex Harvey, and, even though technically it was Lust, a painting of Michelle Pfeiffer as Catwoman. I did do the portrait I mentioned before of Seph, but I never showed it to anybody.

Happiness was just loads of silly paintings of my group of mates, some of which sadly doesn't feature in this story, taken from photographs taken down the pub and the park. Sketches of piles and piles of CD's, books, my favourite foods, musical instruments, and anything that made me happy.

I know some of you may be wondering what Seph and Thys were up to at their time at the college. So I'll side-track once more to tell you. They were studying The History of Art and spent most of their time doing essays about different artists. They would normally choose a famous or not so famous artist. Thys did a piece on Rodin and the end of his project did a modernised version of 'The Kiss,' which was a sculpture of two people in the sexual position known simply as '69'! Fortunately for his tutors, he didn't go into too much detail.

Seph studied the more interesting fellow of Richard Dadd; a very interesting artist indeed, probably more famous for being a murderer though. Let me take a moment to pass off some information, pinched from an art book I have with me, as my own, about Richard Dadd.

Richard Dadd was born in Kent in 1817 and died in 1886.

During the 1840's, people were obsessed with fairy stories and a lot of the artwork that was being produced showed that as an influence. In the 1840's, Dadd and a man called Sir Thomas Phillips travelled through the Middle East and Europe. In Egypt, they met some old Arab men smoking, what they referred to as a 'hubbly-bubbly,' which was a water pipe. Dadd joined the old men and apparently spent five days in a row smoking with them. The men didn't say anything to him, but Dadd thought the noise of the bubbling water pipe was a cryptic message that he unravelled by the fifth day. He believed it to be a calling from the Egyptian god Osiris. In Egyptian mythology, Osiris is murdered and cut into pieces by his brother!

Soon after he had that experience, he started to suffer from frequent headaches and peculiar behaviour. He had symptoms similar to "sunstroke". In Rome, Dadd was overcome with an uncontrollable urge to attack the Pope during a public appearance.

When Dadd returned to England, he was examined by a physician who claimed that he wasn't in sound mind. Instead of being put in an asylum, Dadd persuaded his father that all he needed was a break, and they went to stay in a village in the country called Cobham. Dadd said he would disburden his mind to his father.

Rather than disburden his mind, at a chalk pit, Dadd murdered his father and dismembered him with a knife and razor.

Dadd fled to France where he was caught when he attempted to slash the throat of a tourist. They found a list on him that he'd made of people whom he thought should die, and his father was the first on it.

In his abode in England, they found a sketchbook of all his friends and family, each drawn with their throats slashed.

He was committed to an insane asylum in 1844, where he continued painting. It was whilst in there that he painted his most famous piece of artwork: "Fairy Feller's Master Stroke". The painting is only 21 by 15.5 inches. Even though he spent nine years working on it, he insisted it wasn't finished. It's impossible to do an exact copy of the painting because the layers of paint are so thick that it's practically three-dimensional! He used a magnifying glass to included intricate detail.

He died in 1886 of acute lung disease after being moved to another asylum.

And the moral of that, boys and girls, is to not smoke 'hubbly-bubbly' offered by Arabic men, stick to your cigarettes, super glue, alcohol, and class 'A' drugs!

But hey, let me take you back to the scenario the last chapter ended in.

'As I turned the cold tap on running my hands under the water, I heard an oh so familiar voice, that had earlier that evening featured in a number of flashbacks, say, "Goddard!!!!" Immediately, I sobered up once I looked up into the mirror in front of the sink to see Atkins beside me, his wide mouth exaggerating the grin he had on his face.'

CHAPTER EIGHT

I stared at our reflection in the dirty mirror. An excited expression was painted on his face. Even though I had regressed mentally to my former, shy, scared school-boy self, I nodded a greeting. He jokingly punched me on the shoulder, and I turned to face him beaming down at me. "Hey Goddard, how the hell are you? Lost a bit of weight I see." He said playfully patting my belly.

Somehow, I managed to reply, "Yeah, I'm okay. How are you?"

"I'm great!" His smile faltered, he could tell I was uneasy. "What's wrong?" Then a look of enlightenment sparked across his face as he remembered the endless bullying. "Oh God, fuck!" He covered his face with a hand. He looked down at me, "Oh Jesus man, I am so sorry for all the things I did to you at school. I was an utter cunt then, and I am really sorry." I was amazed, and it must have shown on my face. Also, I discovered that I wasn't frightened of him anymore. "I mean it, I'm really sorry. I'm glad I've bumped into you, you've given me a chance to apologise."

Even though I was suspicious of him, I could tell that he was truly genuine. At first, I was taken aback by his words. I didn't know what to say. After what seemed like minutes, I spoke.

"Okay. I accept your apology. But I can't forget or forgive you for those things you did to me. The best I can do is pretend we've just met and give you a clean slate, mate."

He mulled over my words, smiled his big, awkward Steven Tyler smile and put out a hand for me to shake. "Ok."

I smiled back and shook his hand, "Hi, pleased to meet you, I'm Robert Goddard, but most people call me 'God'."

Atkins chuckled, "My name's Ross Atkins, most people call me Ross, but you can call me 'A Bloody Fucking Wanker'! Let me buy you a drink!" He started to go towards the door, but I held on to his arm.

"Wait a moment, I need to go and explain the situation with the girl I'm with. She knows who you are, and if you go and sit with us without me explaining, she'll fucking disembowel you. Tell you what, if you go and sit where you were, I'll talk to her and beckon you over." Atkins seemed okay with that; he left the toilets and followed by me a few seconds later.

As I walked towards Seph, I could see the look of concern on her face. And rightfully so, she had obviously seen him go into the toilet whilst I was still in there. I was surprised she didn't come in after him and stab him with a stiletto heel. But my Seph never wore stilettos. I sat next to her, reassuring her and told her of the conversation in the toilet and said that part of the reason that I wanted him to come over to our table is that I wanted to see if he had really changed. I also told her that I wasn't afraid of him anymore. She reluctantly agreed to allow him to sit with us, and I waved him over.

The walk he took across the pub must have been a test of endurance under the scrutinizing stare of Seph. He finally got to our table, and before he had a chance to speak, I introduced him to Seph. He shook her hand as Seph muttered a 'hello'. He asked what we were drinking and went to get a round.

"Bastard was eyeing me up good time." Seph said harshly, "I swear, if he makes a move on me, I'll glass him!"

"Well," I smirked uncomfortably, "We could always pretend to be, you know, umm... together?"

Seph giggled a bit and said, "Okay, but no French kissing!"

"What about German fondling?"

Atkins arrived back at the table, drinks in hand, "So," He said, addressing us both. "How do you two know each other?"

We looked at one another, and as I recalled my first encounter with Seph, I said, "We met at college on the first day we started."

A moment to reflect upon this encounter.

The first day of college I was outside the Science block studying the useless little, the badly photocopied layout of the college they had given us to get about the place. The weather was beautiful. As I sat upon the steps to the Science block, the sun shining down on the top of my head, I heard the prettiest, most innocent of voices say 'Oh for fucking cunt's sake, Jesus. Bollocks', and I believe it ended with, 'Arse!' I looked up to see a dark silhouette come between me and the sun's glare. As the figure moved towards me, I saw it be that of Seph. She was wearing white, black, and grey combats and a black vest top with the U.S.S.R hammer and sickle emblem on it.

We gained eye contact, and she stomped over to me. "Hey," She said smiling sweetly, "Do you know where the Art block is? Because this map is just as useful as laminated toilet paper."

I smiled and squinted against the sun, not quite sure why this heavenly angel, with a fiery tongue, that had graced me with her presence wanted to go to the Art block. "Err..." I looked down at the map. "Well... according to this map, it should be here," I said pointing to a square labelled 'Art Block' on the map, "But what actually is there is the..."

"Car park," we both said in unison. We burst into laughter and she gracefully sat beside me on the steps. She held out a red-nail-varnished hand, "I'm Seph, your first day too?"

I shook her hand. "I'm Robert, and yep it's my first day too. What's 'Seph' short for?"

"Hello, Robert. Seph's short for Persephone."

"After the woman in Greek mythology?"

She smirked, a little surprised. "Yeah! So any clue where the Art block is because I've been to the 'car park', and didn't see one easel, let alone a paintbrush."

"Unfortunately, I too am in search of the mythical El Dorado, otherwise known as 'The Art block', and I, like you, do not have the foggiest idea of its whereabouts."

Seph laughed, "So what do you say we should do? You, being a man, are obviously going to be the hero of the day and save me, the damsel in distress, by battling through the evil hordes of Science boffins and Mathematicians to get to our sanctuary."

Finally, I had met someone who could talk improv bullshit too! "Well, companion in the quest for 'The Art Block Of Which All Life's Mysteries Are Contained', I say we must duly make haste to the confines of the tall grey ominous-looking building over there that I have just noticed."

"Why there, oh He of overwhelming courage?"

I smirked at the face of this beautiful girl whom I'd instantly clicked with. "Because, my dear damsel, you are no longer in distress. For on that ominous-looking building is inscribed with the sacred silver plated words of 'Art Block'!" How the hell we didn't notice it was beyond me, but I'm grateful for the shitty map I was given, for if it wasn't for that, I would probably have never met Seph. As it happens, we weren't even in the same class as each other, as I found out after I pulled her up off of the step and we walked to the block.

She had informed me that the class she was ten minutes late for would be finishing at three, and if I was available then to meet her on the steps so we could 'go and get served in some dodgy pub that serves under-agers!' she would be waiting. And so a beautiful friendship began.

Back to The Golden Lion: I had just told Atkins me and Seph met on our first day at college, remember?

"Oh great, that's cool." He said enthusiastically. Maybe he had turned religious and was trying to make up for his wicked past. The conversation wound on and on with me and Atkins talking about High School, but obviously not 'certain incidences'. He asked Seph a lot of questions, to which she gave as little an answer as possible. We all got pretty inebriated as the night went on, and I learnt that Atkins had left school to go to college and finally become an Accountant and that his hobbies included: playing football, going rock-climbing, playing on his game console and watching television.

The night drew on and nature roared at Seph to empty her bladder, and I was left alone with Atkins. As soon as Seph had gone, he leaned close to me, his breath, like mine, most probably reeking of beer, and said. "You've done well there mate." He meant Seph. I just smiled and nodded. He drained his latest bottle and leaned forward again. "So how long have you been a 'couple' then, since you met?" This is where I cocked up slightly.

"Oh, it's our second date."

He looked confused for a second. "So you were mates then you, you know…?"

"Yeah, sort of."

He looked over his shoulder to see if Seph was returning. She wasn't. "I hope you don't mind me asking, but is she, you know, giving out? She looks kind of frigid."

I tried not to be annoyed at this comment, and I succeeded. "No, she's not like that, Seph believes in waiting for the right time."

He must have thought I meant that in a negative way because he sympathetically said, "Aww mate that's no good." He was remarkably drunk, but I don't think that counted for the way he spoke. Most stereotypical blokes talk like that, treating women like sexual objects. Looking about still, he reached into his pocket and pulled something out and hid it in his hand. Whispering, "Listen, this is just between you and me, call it a way to make up for all the shit I put you through at school. Here…" He put whatever he removed from his pocket in my hand. "It'll give her a kick-start!"

I looked at the small glass vial that he'd put in my hand, it contained a tablet. Even though I guessed what it was, I still wanted it confirmed, "What's this?"

"Roofies ain't it? Rohypnol!" He said voice even quieter. Before I had a chance to chuck it in his face, Seph came back, so I quickly hid the vial in my pocket.

As she sat down, I stood up to go to the bar. On the way, I winked at Atkins and patted him on the shoulder. It's funny; the situation could have gone many ways. One: I could have thrown the Rohypnol in his face and exposed him for what he had given me in front of the whole pub. Two: I could have accepted it and actually spiked Seph's drink with it, so I could have my wicked way with her. I must add that didn't cross my mind. Or Three: I could have walked off and discreetly telephoned the police.

I chose the fourth option. I stood at the bar, which I must say was shaped like a horseshoe. One end visible to the main part of the pub where Seph and Atkins were, and the other end in the quieter, practically empty lounge area where I got served. I had two pints of lager, a bottle of Budweiser on the beer-soaked bar top before me, and a vial containing Rohypnol hidden in my palm. When I left the bar, it was minus the contents of the vial.

CHAPTER NINE

We sat, us three, Atkins and me reminiscing about High School, but still skating around the danger area. Every now and then, he'd give me a knowing wink. Within about half an hour, Atkins began to act strangely. His head kept nodding forward, and he kept sitting up with a start and kept saying, "God, I'm pissed, man!"

Seph rolled her eyes and beckoned towards the door. I knew she wanted to be away from his company, so did I. I leant forward and put a hand on his shoulder to wake him up. Atkins lashed out at me and shoved my hand away shouting a slurred, "Get off!" Seph and I both stood up. Atkins looked up apologetically. I could tell by the look of his eyes that he was having trouble focusing. "I'm sorry mate," He said as if I were an actual friend, "It's just... oh shit, I think I'm going to be sick!" I don't know why, but I sort of felt sorry for him, so I helped him to his feet and much to Seph's surprise, I supported him into the toilets.

"Hold on mate, we're nearly in there" I reassured him as we walked across the tiled floor. I managed to kick open a cubicle door and attempted to steer him into the cubicle, but he collapsed suddenly and I lost grip on him. He lay on his front on the pissy-wet floor making a gurgling noise. I bent down and lifted him under the arms. Atkins knelt there for about a second before throwing up. I ran out of the way of the puddle of vomit and stood behind him. I heard someone enter the toilets and saw the look on the guy's face that entered.

"Aww, fucking hell! That's put me off getting a kebab tonight." He half-joked to me when he saw Atkins hunched over heaving.

"I'm just glad he missed me!" I said laughing, "Any chance you can give me a hand getting him up?"

The man grimaced and reluctantly said, "Hang on, let me have a piss then I'll give you a hand." The man pissed his piss then said, "Righto." We both grabbed an arm and got Atkins to his feet. "You alright chief?" The man asked Atkins.

Atkins focused slightly and nodded. "You think you can stand alright?" Atkins nodded again. The man looked at me, doubtful, and we let go. Atkins just stood there with a glazed expression on his face.

"Cheers," I thanked the man, and addressing Atkins, "Can you walk okay?" Atkins nodded. As the man turned to go to the door, Atkins took a step and slid in the puddle of sick he'd made. "Shit," I cried as his feet went from under him and he fell over backwards. On the way down, he smashed his head hard on one of the urinals, and it made a sickening sound on its impact on the floor.

The man immediately crouched down next to Atkins and lifted his head. A dark pool of blood flowed freely from the back of his head. Straight away I removed my shirt and pressed it to the wound and sat supporting his head on my lap.

"I'll get someone to call an ambulance!" The man shouted and ran from the toilets. I was on my own with Atkins. It didn't surprise me at the time, but Atkins was conscious. I would have thought that a knock as hard as the one he'd suffered would have knocked him out. He mumbled something to me, but at first, I couldn't understand him. And as I'd seen them do it on hospital programs when people have head injuries I thought I'd better talk to him to keep him conscious. That said, I remember feeling a little tired and odd myself. I realise now that was due to the effect of the Rohypnol I'd spiked my own drink with.

So anyway, I tried to keep him awake, even though I felt like I was going to fall asleep at any moment. "What did you say, mate?" He moaned in pain and then repeated himself.

"I said…. Who would have thought, three years ago, that I'd be sitting here with my head caved in with you, you fat fuck!" I was shocked by his sudden outburst.

"It's not my fault your fucking head's bleeding! You got yourself into this state!" Atkins tried to move away from me, but I held him still. If he were to move, the shirt I was using to pad the bleeding would have come away. He didn't like being restricted.

"Get off me you cunt. I know what you've done, you fat bastard. You've given me the fucking Rohypnol!" He ceased struggling and looked up at me and whispered. "I know what you've done." I gazed down at his whitening face and smiled at him, revelling in the look of horror in his eyes.

"Now why would I want to do a thing like that?" As I finished my sentence, I lifted his head up a bit more and let go of him and my bloody shirt. Atkins fell back onto the floor again, his head bashing on the tiles once again. I lifted him up again and put my shirt behind his head and cradled him. Atkins was unconscious. It was then that I felt really, really weird indeed. It took all the strength I could muster to place the empty Rohypnol vial carefully in his trouser pocket. I felt incredibly weak. The last thing I remember before I blacked out was the man who had helped me with Atkins rushing into the toilets and saying that an ambulance was on its way.

I think I was unconscious for about four hours altogether. I recall reading a list of side effects that Rohypnol can have on people after I took it:

Under Rohypnol, individuals may experience a slowing of psychomotor performance, muscle relaxation, decreased blood pressure, sleepiness, and/or amnesia. Some of the adverse side effects associated with the drug's use are drowsiness, headaches, memory impairment, dizziness, nightmares, confusion, and tremors.

I don't think I suffered from amnesia, I can't remember. Ba-doom-tish! But I know the drug, well at least I think it was the drug, gave me a really fucked-up dream. It was so vivid and so graphically horrific!

I remember opening my eyes and being back in the front row at an Alex Harvey concert like I dreamt after killing Stuart. I don't recall what he was singing, but I do remember that the band was putting on some sort of 'act' as they were performing, which was the band's trademark back in the day. Alex was prancing about the stage, crooning in his broad Scottish accent. He was wearing his trademark black and white striped jumper but wore what looked like a German Second World War Nazi uniform, complete with red swastika armband and a rifle with fixed bayonet. I don't know how accurate my mind was with the finer details, as I don't know what the German weaponry was like, but that is what he carried.

Zal Cleminson, the guitarist, was dressed head to toe in a sporty white tracksuit, topped off with a Burberry baseball cap. He always wore clown make-up on stage, and this was no exception, the whiteness of his face making his painted red lips more obvious; his painted red lips exaggerated his over-sized mouth and extreme facial expressions.

The backdrop of the stage was just a park bench and brickwork. At the back of the stage, a man, who I recognised to be the band's drummer, held up a hand-painted sign with a big yellow 'M' on it. It was then that I realised what it was they were portraying. Zal was walking on the spot, miming talking into a brick-sized mobile phone, while Alex crept, rifle jutting out in front of him. Their movements were so embellished it was like some bizarre pantomime. Both of them walking on the spot, Zal's clown-face speaking and laughing silently on the phone, and Alex looking mean, snarling the lyrics through gritted teeth.

Then he stopped singing and unscrewed the bayonet from his rifle to a dramatic sound effect. Zal turned around and saw Alex. His clown-face erupting into uncontrollable silent laughter, his hands holding his stomach, which was shaking with the spasms. His expression changed from humour to horror as Alex threw a fake punch at Zal's face. I could see it missed by a least a few inches; however, blood exploded from Zal's nose in a ridiculous fountain that sprayed and splattered the audience.

That was another weird thing, the audience found this hysterical, and when I turned to look at them, I found I was the only one sitting there, despite the room full of laughter! I watched, more than slightly disturbed, as Zal re-enacted Stuart's move by putting Alex in a headlock. Zal's make-up had gone pinkish around the mouth and nose due to the blood. The invisible audience cheered, hollered, and whistled as Alex brought the bayonet across Zal's stomach. A colossal geyser of blood completely covered me. The look of pain and fear on Zal's face mirrored that of Stuart's and seemed absolutely genuine. Alex walked away from Zal, dropping the bayonet, and looked slightly shocked as he started singing again. Zal fell back onto the park bench, looking bloody and pale.

A spotlight shone down on Alex, the rest of the stage dark behind him. He fell to his knees and looked down at me as he sung the only few sentences of the song I can remember, "Why did I do it? What went wrong? Should I call for help? Should I just run away? Will I rot in a cell for a hundred years, never to get the love that I so desperately crave?"

He looked mournfully down at me, then lowered his head and sighed. Another spotlight shone down on Zal slumped on the bench, phone in his hand. Alex stood up smiling, bayonet in hand. He ran and skipped over to Zal, grabbed a handful of his curly black hair, exposing his throat. He sang a few more sentences and then brought the knife across Zal's throat. As he did, the lights were extinguished and I woke up with the biggest headache ever.

CHAPTER TEN

As I said in the most riveting closure of the last chapter, 'I woke up with the biggest headache ever'. Well yeah, it was a big 'un, and my head did feel as though it was being slowly squeezed in an ancient, rusty old iron vice, like the one my old next-door neighbour once had in his little green shed that constantly smelt of White Spirits and paint. God, I used to love going down there and watching him make stuff out of, get this, wood!

Anyway, I'm drifting off into the dark realms of reminiscence; duly forgive me as I have just consumed a few bottles of a must-try Belgian beer called Bush. I bet that's fucked with your heads now, suddenly blasting into present tense! Sorry, Bush beer aside, and on with the show. Head in a vice, remember?

Obviously, I wasn't surprised to wake up in a hospital bed, but even though I did expect it, I was still surprised to see Seph sat beside me, or should I mention, asleep in the horrid-looking leatherette green armchair that crouched beside the bed. I inwardly swooned when I saw her, and seeing her beautiful sleeping face was all I needed to extinguish the foul throbbing of my head. I noticed that she had been crying, as her black mascara had run in streaks down her cheeks and made her appear like an Alice Cooper fan. In a way, I hated to see that she had been weeping, but I secretly hoped that those tears were for me.

I must have sat there for a full ten minutes, happily watching her sleep, until she woke up and saw me. Within an instant, she jumped up and took me by the hand and gazed down with a concerned look on her face. "Are you okay?"

I nodded and squeezed her hand. She lowered her eyes and bit her lip; there was something on her mind. "Umm Atkins...."

"Oh shit!" I cursed as if I had forgotten about his little 'accident.' "Is he okay?" Seph gazed in the direction of the clock on the wall.

"He died about an hour and a half ago." Fuck! I thought I've done it again! I wondered whether it would be taken the wrong way if I was to leap up out of the bed and do a one-man Mexican Wave. I decided against it, besides, Seph's next sentence chilled me to the very core. "The Police want to talk with you." My blood froze and cold beads of sweat started forming on my forehead. I'll be amazed if I didn't look guilty there and then.

"Err. What do they want to speak with me for?"

"Oh God, don't worry, they don't think you beat him up or anything," She laughed dryly. "They've spoken to the guy who called the ambulance and they just want you to verify the info, that's all. Chill out." I breathed a fake sigh of relief.

"The poor bastard."

"Who Atkins? Huh, he deserved it the twat!" Seph snapped and moved away to the green chair. "Fucking spiking your drink, the cunt!"

"Oh thank fuck for that! I was wondering why I blacked out, thought I'd got a tumour the size of Walthamstow in my head!"

Seph smirked. "Nope Rohypnol I'm afraid!"

"Fuck, no? I was given the date rape drug! Do you think he was gonna, you know, force me to participate in some packing of the confectionary known as 'fudge'?" I said shocked.

Seph burst out laughing, and then shushed herself when she realised where she was. "He didn't come across as a fudgepacker." Then on a more serious note, "Especially the way he was looking down my cleavage all night. I honestly don't know what he was playing at. Probably just having a 'laugh', the silly bastard!"

"I'm still shocked, I mean when I saw him, I was just instantly zapped back to High school with him towering over me. When he came in the toilets, I almost shit myself. But he was very convincing with all his apologies and everything. I should've known he'd end up being a cunt. He always used to do stuff like that at school, you know, be nice to me for a few days, and then show me up in front of the whole class or something. I honestly thought he had grown up. What a silly knob."

"Look, you weren't to know okay. Yeah, you should've told him to 'fuck off' as soon as he even breathed near you, but that's not you. You're the gentlest person ever, and you're better than that. You gave him a chance to reconcile his misgivings, and he was the one who fucked it up."

I was about to say something when there was a knock on the door and a moustachioed Policeman poked his head around. "Ah, Mr Goddard, you're awake! May I come in?"

I smiled and nodded. I didn't like the look of the Policeman; he was ridiculously tall with thinning brown hair and a thin-lipped mouth that was hard to see behind his frighteningly bushy brush-like moustache. Plus, just the way he spoke reminded me of some Colombo-type detective, the one who knew the famous celebrity who's cameo-ing in the episode is the one who did the murder purely because it's the only famous celebrity cameo-ing in that episode. Soon, I thought, he's going to start asking me questions that are hard to lie to and I'm going to suddenly scream out 'Ahhhhh! I killed Ross Atkins and while I'm at it, I killed a chav called Stuart. How did you figure it out Colombo, you one-eyed, hunchbacked freak?'

"Do you mind, Miss, if myself and Mr Goddard could speak privately for a few minutes?" The Policeman said courteously to Seph.

Seph smirked sympathetically at me and got up to go. "See you in a bit."

"Look, why don't you go home mate, you need sleep, haven't you got work?" I said wondering why I was pretending that I wanted her to leave me.

"Ah, work schmirk!! I ain't going home without you babe. I'll go get a coffee and come back this way in a bit." She spun around and walked out the door leaving me truly touched by the fact that she wanted to stay with me.

The Policeman smiled at me. "Ah, she's a charming young lady. Allow me to introduce myself, Mr Goddard, I'm $%^&*£?@" I had a momentary mind-freeze then and can't for the life of me remember the Policeman's name. So for the sake of my not wanting to continue writing 'the policeman...' Etc.... etc.... etc.... I shall call him PC Fawlty because he bore a vague semblance to John Cleese's Fawlty Towers character Basil Fawlty.

I really hated the way he kept saying my name, it made me feel nervous, as though I was being interrogated by the Inquisition, or a James Bond villain. I just smiled uncomfortably and muttered light-heartedly, "Well you know who I am" PC Fawlty chuckled slightly, "Well that is indeed true. How are you feeling? I expect you have a killer of a headache?"

I grimaced, "Yes, it's a bad one alright." And it's getting a whole lot worse now I've got to be hassled by you, I said to him using my defunct telepathic powers.

Worrisomely enough, he seemed to read my mind as his actual next line was: "I suppose me keeping you awake at this hour won't help matters, I'll not keep you long." He cleared his throat and withdrew the trademark Policeman's Notebook from within his coat pocket. He scribbled something on the notebook and began. "So, would you like to tell me what happened, Mr Goddard?"

I hesitated at first, trying to get all the details in my head. Unfortunately, the Rohypnol hadn't given me memory loss, for it would have been an easy way out. "Well, me and Seph went to this pub because there was supposed to be a school reunion for my High School leavers. We sat there for ages and the only person I remember turning up apart was Ross Atkins. At first, he didn't see me and sat on the other side of the pub." I paused and reached for the glass of water that was on the cabinet beside the bed. "Sorry, dry throat..." The water was lukewarm, but it served its purpose. "When I saw him, I was tempted to leave because he used to bully me in High school and I hated him."

"What made you stay?" Fawlty said, stroking his moustache. With a moustache like that, it'd be a crime not to stroke it whilst deep in thought.

"Well, this is a bit embarrassing…" I eyed the door to make sure that Seph hadn't suddenly come back. "You see, I've sort of got a thing, a crush on Seph…"

"Sorry, 'Seph'? That's the girl who was with you?" Fawlty said, interrupting me.

I nodded. "Yeah, well I didn't want to go home, I was enjoying being out with her, it was like being on a date, even though it wasn't, you know what I mean? So, seeing as Atkins was the other side of the pub, I thought I'd stay. Then, a while after he came in, I went to the toilets and saw him in there."

PC Fawlty sat listening intently. "Did he recognise you?"

"Yeah, he did. He was really astounded. He started apologising about all the crap he'd put me through at school and was on about how he wanted to make it up to me. So for some reason, I believed him and allowed him to sit with us. I was really wary of him, but I thought that he would have grown up by now. Anyway, we sat for at least an hour and a half, and for about fifteen minutes before Atkins suddenly said he was going to be sick, I felt really tired and really drunk. But I helped him to the toilets where he collapsed. I tried to help him up, but then he was sick all over the floor.

"That's when the guy who called the ambulance came in. He helped me lift Atkins up and we made sure he was okay and got him to his feet. We asked him if he was okay to stand, and he,

Atkins, said that he was. I know that we shouldn't have trusted his judgement, but there you go, we let him go. That was when he slipped on his vomit and cracked his head against the urinal, and then the floor. Oh, Jesus!"

I put my hands over my face. "God the sound it made and the blood. I didn't know whether to move him or not; you know, sometimes it's dangerous to move people. But the other man lifted his head up and it was bleeding really bad. I took off my shirt and held it against the wound. The other guy went to call for an ambulance, and I knelt beside him and cradled his head."

PC Fawlty made a 'hmmm' noise and took his hand away from his moustache to speak. "You say his head hit the urinal and then the floor?" Oh fuck, I thought, what the fuck have I said. I slowly nodded. It's moments like these when Colombo moves in for the kill. "Ah, so you are the famous celebrity guest starring in this episode! I'm sorry I don't watch much television, I'm afraid. We had Johnny Cash last week, had to string the questioning out for ages. I'm a huge fan you see. As soon as I saw him playing a new preacher in town, I knew he'd murdered someone! Hahahaha. So you killed Atkins?"

"You see the pathologist who had a look at Mr Atkins seemed to believe that his head had been repeatedly hit against the tiled floor, at least three times in fact." On the outside, I tried to look confused, but on the inside, I was terrified.

"Umm, well I don't think he hit it anymore. The last thing I can remember before I passed out was the other guy coming in and saying something. Oh, God!"

PC Fawlty sat forward, eyes wide, "What is it?"

"I hope I didn't drop his head when I passed out, oh shit!"

"I believe that is most probably the case, Mr Goddard. But it is nothing for you to feel concerned about. One of the symptoms of Rohypnol is muscle relaxation, so you were most probably not in control during the last few moments before you collapsed. Well, you've been most helpful Mr Goddard; I shan't take up any more of your time, as I can see you need to sleep." Fawlty stood up, shook my hand and just as he turned towards the door, he turned back.

"Oh, I am sorry, just one other thing. We found the vial of Rohypnol in Mr Atkins' pocket; just as a precautionary, we dusted it for prints. Can you tell me how it came to have his and your fingerprints on it?" Hah! I was expecting this question!

"Umm... earlier in the evening, whilst Seph was in the toilet, Atkins started quizzing me on my and Seph's sexual relations. I don't know why, but I told him that we hadn't had sex. That was when he gave me the vial of what he told me was Rohypnol."

"And how did you react to that?" Fawlty asked.

"I was polite, even though I was really shocked by the fact that he had the drug in the first place. I wanted to tell him where to go and throw the vial. But I was polite and just said that I was dead against that sort of thing and handed the vial back to him, so he put it back in his pocket. I think that pissed him off, so I suspect he put it in my drink, as he bought the majority of the drinks after that."

Fawlty smiled beneath his big Magnum moustache, "Thank you for clearing that up for me. Good night, Mr Goddard, I hope you feel better soon." I muttered an appreciative 'thank you' and said 'goodbye'.

A few minutes after PC Fawlty left, Seph came into the room. She had cleaned the streaked mascara from her face, along with the rest of her make-up. I could see that she ached for sleep as much I did, but I ached for her a lot more than anything else. She came in and slumped into the green armchair.

"So what did Brush-Face have to say for himself?" I smirked at her nickname for him.

"Nothing much, really. I just went through everything that happened, and that's it really." I couldn't tell her about the fact I had known about the Rohypnol earlier in the night.

"That's alright then. God, I need sleep." She said via a humongous yawn. I could see that her eyelids were beginning to droop. Seph rested her folded arms on my thigh and rested her face on them. She smiled at me and then shut her eyes. Within seconds, she was asleep. My mind played over the acts of the night, the many pathways that it could've gone down. Never would I have given the Rohypnol to Seph, never. I would rather suffer from the hurt of a broken heart for all eternity than ever violate her in such a way. I lightly brushed my fingers through her long, red hair and stroked the side of her face. She startled me by kissing my hand, smiling again, and falling back asleep. I kept my hand cupped against her face until I fell asleep.

I fell asleep wondering what the kiss meant. I wondered if it was a sign that she felt something more than just friendship for me. Was I ever going to get that lucky?

CHAPTER ELEVEN

One thing that didn't add up with me, that crossed my mind about my interview with Fawlty, was that I just didn't believe that the police would have autopsy and fingerprint results from Atkins in such a short time! I believe that he thought there may have been something more sinister going on. You see, he had already spoken to Seph about what had happened, and she had told him about Atkins being a total twat, that he used to treat me like shit at school. I think that Fawlty thought he'd be clever by throwing a few imaginary fishing lines out to see what he could catch. I fell for them, good and proper, as he made some very good guesses. But you can rest assured; I didn't hear anything else from Fawlty, or anyone else for that matter, which I kind of find hard to believe also. A strange turn of events indeed.

Anyway, when I awoke later that morning, I was so pleased to see that Seph was still by my side. Unfortunately, she was no longer resting upon my leg, but she was curled up in a ball on the green armchair, and I praised the lord up above for the amount of fishnet-clad thigh she was showing. Obviously, I feasted my eyes upon this but was careful not to get caught. As soon as I noticed her stir, I faked sleep.

I heard her yawn and stretch out and heard her shuffle about in the chair. I awoke and looked up, groggily, at her face. "Mrng" I mumbled in gibberish. It's a well-known fact that no man, without exception, can form actual words first thing in the morning. We must communicate via Neanderthal-like grunts and by pointing at things we want. Whereas all women, without exception, are capable of having a full conversation about anything as soon as they wake up before the soapy water of the previous night's dreams spirals and twirls down the metaphysical plughole of that special kind of dream/amnesia.

Seph attempted a two-way conversation with me, but gave up and just told me what had happened the night before, and how Fawlty had interviewed her also. After about thirty minutes of being awake, some doctor came and said I could 'go home' so go home I did.

I got a day off sick from the fuck-awful supermarket. I really didn't want to tell them the reason why I was off, as the fact that I'd been given the 'date rape' drug would no doubt have caused all the workers there to find something else to rip the piss out of me about. So, I just told them I was sick. I'm shit at making up excuses for skiving. The only ones that I use, when obviously not genuinely ill, are always either vomiting or a-really-bad-flu-like-disease-that-will-probably-last-at-least-until-the-time-I-would-have-left-work-had-I-gone-to-work-disease-ridden-and-then-miraculously-recover-incase-you-see-me-down-the-pub and saying that I appear to have all the symptoms of a really bad hangover. Which is often caused by excessive consumption of alcohol. But Seph kept me company all day whilst the guys were at work, and we just vegged in our PJ's watching crappy horror films and drinking cheap Tesco pop.

I grudgingly went back to the supermarket the next day. I arrived and followed my usual routine. I avoided the cackles of the witches and the filthy guffaws that emanated from the staff room. I went into the men's toilets, where they, fortunately, kept the lockers, took my Stanley knife out of my bag, and slung my bag in the locker. Then I made to walk past the staff room when I was spotted as I walked past the door.

"Oi Goddard!" Someone shouted out. I chose to ignore it, but the caller came out of the room. It was a guy in his early forties named Steve, one of the warehouse supervisors. He looked quite young for his age and had fashionable short-spiky hair and had a monthly direct debit for the local gym, although I think he only used it for the solarium. Apparently, he was the most fancied man in the shop. Everyone saw him as a cheeky, outgoing joker-type. I saw him as a total bastard.

He beckoned me over, taking a second to cast a glance over his shoulder to grin cheesily and wink at his audience in the staff room. I turned slightly to look in his direction. "What?"

Steve grinned slyly at me. "Oh I was just wondering if you were feeling better today, that's all."

"I'm fine, thank you," I said slightly civil. I turned and walked down the stairs to the shop floor, leaving the bursts of hysterical laughter echoing behind me. I really didn't understand that at all. I desperately needed to escape this foul place and get employment in a better establishment, with more intelligent staff. Niv was constantly keeping an ear open for vacancies at HMV, and even Thys and Seph were also listening for news of vacancies. But to be honest, I didn't think that working with mates as well as living with them would be a good thing. Surely conversation would run dry. As much as I'd have loved to spend all the time I have with Seph, the idea of working in a pub didn't attract me anymore.

It was when I started loading up a cage with boxes of biscuits that I decided what I wanted to do. For the previous, however many months, years, I was besotted with Seph. I knew that if I was to remain in such close contact with her, I would just torture myself until eventually; she would find someone again and move away. I couldn't go on like this. I knew I'd never had the courage to put our friendship in jeopardy by confessing my undying love for her. So when Nivek's mum came into the warehouse, with her coven, and said upon spotting me with a large box of McVitie's' Chocolate Digestives in my hands, "Oh that's just his breakfast that is!" I made my mind up to, not just get out of the supermarket, not just get out of town, but get out of England altogether.

As I mentioned a few chapters back, Nivek and Kol'n were saving to travel across Europe, and originally, I had been tempted to join them, but the thought of not being in the same country as Seph didn't sound too good. But I thought that the best thing to get me away from the burning unrequited love I had for her was, as hard as it sounds, to get away from her. Whilst I scowled at Nivek's mum, I knew my plan of action.

I somehow managed to get through yet another day without killing Niv's mum and came home to interrupt Niv and Kol'n being rather intimate on the sofa in our living-room, which was convenient. Fortunately, they weren't getting down to anything serious, but I did feel a slight pang of jealousy at the fact that I'd caught yet another one of my mates in the throes of passion. When was it going to be my turn? They looked up, slightly embarrassed, and moved to opposite ends of the sofa from one another.

"Oh, don't mind me," I said, collapsing into the nearest armchair. "Just don't go leaving teeth marks on the cushions!" Kol'n sniggered and Nivek just rolled his eyes awkwardly. "Actually, I'm glad you two are in. There was something I wanted to ask you."

Nivek chilled out a bit, "What do you want to know, mate? What sort of lubrication do we use? Who is the 'giver'? Who is the 'receiver'?" I grimaced at his words. It wasn't that I was homophobic; I just didn't want to dwell on the intricate details of homosexuality and its sexual practices.

"Right, well, you know, Niv that I'm really fed up with my job for obvious reasons." Niv looked at me guiltily. "And I'm more than fed up with this town. I was wondering, I mean, you can tell me to fuck off, I will understand, whether I could tag along with you two when you travel Europe at the end of the term?" For a few seconds, there was total silence, and then Nivek's face broke into the biggest smile ever.

"That'd be fucking awesome mate!!" And so it was agreed. I should've known better at the time, I should have let him and Kol'n go off and discuss things before he gave me an answer. Things wouldn't have gone wrong then.

CHAPTER TWELVE

A few days after I had asked Nivek about joining him and Kol'n on their European adventure, I decided to tidy my bedroom. The dust in there was getting quite bad, and I felt ashamed of myself as I had normally always been quite a tidy person. It was whilst cleaning my room that I happened upon Stuart's (Remember? The mugger man who kicked the shit out of me and went out with Seph) mobile phone. As it was the same model as mine, I disposed of the original fascia and put one of my spare ones on it. After doing that, I just threw it in the corner of my wardrobe.

I don't know what made me do it, but I switched the phone on. The yellow screen flashed to life, and I toggled on the menu and to the pictures section. I automatically skipped through the pictures of Page Three Girls, football emblems, and other crap, until I came to the picture of me lying on the war monument, all battered and bruised. Seeing this roused a streak of vengeance that had lain dormant since I ended Stuart's life.

The job wasn't quite finished yet.

I flicked through the pictures and stopped at the one of Jez, Stuart's mate and my other mugger. I quickly scoured the phone's directory and found Jez's mobile and home number. I jotted these down and lay on my bed with my phone in my hand. Still, in autopilot, I rang Jez's mobile number.

"I'm sorry this number is no longer in use, goodbye" Came the answer at the other end. It made sense; most young people go through mobile phones like monkeys go through bananas. So I tried his home phone. I must hasten to add, I was obviously withholding my own number. A woman answered she had the usual broad Suffolk accent.

"Yeah, who is it?"

For a few seconds, I was stumped for what to say, and the words just came out of my mouth. "Can I speak to Jez?"

"You're not fucking speaking to no-one if you're not telling me who you are. So say your name, or piss off!" The charming lady told me.

I was silent for another second or two, I heard the woman shout something to a screaming kid in the background. Then I spoke, "Now you listen here, you fucking bitch, I know where you live, so you better listen to what I have to say, or I'll take it out on that kid of yours, believe me, I will!" I shocked myself and prayed to God that no one else in my house could hear me. To make sure, I kept my voice to a low menacing growl.

The woman didn't say anything, but I could tell I had her undivided attention. "Now, I'm a mate of Skinner's," The gang leader who was arrested for Stuart's murder, "And I know that Jez stitched him up."

"I don't know anything about it," The woman said abruptly. "I've only been going out with him for a bit!"

"Well listen very carefully, I shall say this only once," Do you remember the Second World War 80's sitcom ALLO, ALLO? I almost burst into laughter there and then. "Tell Jez to meet me outside The Baker's Oven," Not the most tough-sounding of meeting points. You wouldn't get James Bond-type spies meeting in such places. ("Blue Fox, the location for the rendezvous will be at nineteen hundred hours, outside Gregg's.") "Next Thursday night at a quarter to twelve. If he's not there by twelve, me and the boys will pay you a house-visit!"

The woman didn't say anything for at least a minute, but I could hear her writing something down. "If I tell him that you're a mate of Skinner's, then he'll do a runner." Obviously, she had lied about 'not knowing anything about it'.

"Then don't tell him! Just make sure he's there. Maybe you two could arrange a nice night out?" I said sarcastically.

"If..." the woman began, "If I get him there at that time and place, can you promise not to hurt me or my kid?"

"He is the only one we've got an issue with. You won't be harmed. I promise." I said reassuringly. I hung up after she had agreed to get Jez at his destination. Even though I remember everything I said it was as if someone else was inside of me controlling my speech. I was slightly scared but also excited about this other side of my personality. I was, by far, a lot braver and cockier than the man I was before my attack.

The question I asked myself was what do I want Jez to be outside The Baker's Oven for? I sat and thought about what I was going to do next. When I had decided, I stood and looked at myself in front of the mirror in my wardrobe. I realised a trip to the charity shop would be required. What I had planned to do was one of the most stupid, dangerous things I've ever done, then.

There's always the same smell, feel, and atmosphere when you go into charity shops in my town. As soon as you enter, a combination of musk, old clothes, and death hits you. I'm not a snob, I have been known to make purchases in these kinds of shops, but I always feel uncomfortable for some reason. The places are usually crammed with old people who all seem to know one another. Rails upon rails of unwanted and dead people's clothes hang to be fingered and snatched up by the charity shop connoisseur. And that's before you get to the people who work in there. Apart from the occasional sexy, young American, most of the staff tends to be old and grumpy, or young, inbred-looking, and amazingly stupid.

Most charity shops boast a vast collection of books and CD's to entice the younger generation to enter and see what treasures they can find, but once you actually get to the solitary shelf containing the 'vast' collection, you realise that all it comprises of are Reader's Digest Friendship Books, and the majority of the CD's are by artists such as Lionel Richie and Fun Boy Three, not that there's anything wrong with Fun Boy Three, bless Terry Hall, God rest his soul [not that he's dead yet. Well not at the time of writing this anyway]. As for Lionel Richie...

But like I said, this is what the charity shops were like in my town, they may be different elsewhere, but I doubt it very much.

So on this bright, bright, bright, sunshiny day, I ventured into my nearest charity shop, the one that gives money to animals. I walked past the fur coats and leather handbags, up to the men's section. I gazed over the rails of bad shirts, corduroy trousers, pullovers, and other such things that are mainly fashionable to the over sixty until I found something along the lines of which I was looking for. About fifteen minutes later I left the charitable shop with a Sainsbury's bag (Because they don't have their own) full of clothing. I was quite chuffed really, as I had got a whole outfit for no more than six pounds! Cheap at half the price! I'll never understand that saying.

As soon as I got home, I tried on my brand new, second-hand outfit and stood to look at myself in the mirror, slightly sickened by what I saw. I shall describe, in scintillating detail, my outfit from my feet up. Upon my feet were the hideous white Puma trainers; they were covered in scuff marks but were wearable. Above these, I wore, for the first time since I was about six years old, some tracksuit trousers. They were blue with a white stripe running down the legs saying, 'Adidas', they were big enough but hot and irritating. On top of this, I had found a white hoodie which had 'Le Coq Sportif' emblazoned upon it. I don't know how people can walk around with 'the sporting cock' written on them! I wore the hood up and had a genuine, fake Burberry baseball cap, that I was overwhelmed with finding.

I just could not get over how lucky I was in my purchases. I highly recommend charity shops! I considered seeing if I could find some dodgy gold jewellery from somewhere, a few sovereign rings, a couple of thick gold chains, but I didn't want to go overboard. With the hood up and cap on, I managed to hide all of my hair, and I looked one-hundred percent Chav.

The plan I had in mind was to scour Christchurch Park and find and infiltrate the same gang that Skinner had been head of. That was if they still existed. But I thought once a petty crim, always a petty crim.

Leaving the house one evening at about eight, I left Seph looking slightly perplexed as to where I was going on my own. As painful as it was, I had tried desperately to avoid her ever since I made my decision to go to Europe with Niv and Kol'n. I obviously told her about my plans to travel, to which she didn't say much apart from, "Well, if it's what you want..." My avoiding her had given her a complex that she had upset me in some way, and she started to appear slightly inhibited. When she asked me where I was going, I just said, "Out," and left.

On the way to the park, I stopped off in a little Irish pub for some Dutch-courage. Why do they call it that? I got a few looks in there because I was on my own and also because I was about forty years younger than most of the other patrons who were propped up against the bar. After I had had about four pints of cider, I took my backpack into the toilet and changed into 'Chavvy Goddard'. I can tell you, I got, even more, stares when I came out of the toilet dressed in a total new style of clothing.

I asked the barman if there was any chance he'd allow me to leave my bag behind the bar until later that night, or the next day if I gave him a few pounds. He agreed that I could, but did not accept my money.

The park was opposite the pub, and I could see that, by now, the main gates were locked. But almost everyone knew that there was an easy way to get into the park after hours. I walked up the road that ran up the side of the park, following the ancient red-bricked wall and rusted railing, until I came to a certain point. There was a huge, thick tree-stump that stood about three feet tall. The fence and wall stopped about nine inches either side of it. I squeezed through the gap and entered the murky park. I walked across the black grass in almost pitch-darkness. It took my eyes a few minutes to adjust to the lack of light and to get my bearings.

Once I'd figured out where I was, I headed towards the public toilets—the infamous spot for users and apparently where prostitutes took their clientele. I started to feel quite anxious when I spotted the dim, orange glow of the light bulbs illuminating the entrance to the toilets and the shadowy figures lurking thereabouts. It was then that I almost considered turning around and running like hell.

CHAPTER THIRTEEN

I adjusted my baseball cap and hood as I approached the public toilets. As I got closer, I could see that the figures in the doorway of a man and woman. The woman was kneeling before him, participating in a sexual act. Try as I did to avoid looking too much, I heard the man shout, 'What the fuck are you looking at?'

I carried on, past the couple, and sat on an empty bench out of their view. I felt really scared and overwhelmingly hot sitting there in my chav clothes, bathed in orange light. I didn't know how long I was going to wait, or what I was going to do or say.

After about two minutes, I heard the stifled groan of the man in the toilet doorway, and then heard the sound of the woman he was with spitting on the ground. My stomach churned as I watched the man walk past, giving me a filthy look. He mumbled something under his breath as he walked by. His lady of the night stood outside with her back to me, applying some makeup with a small round mirror. It must've been whilst she was doing this that she noticed me sitting on the bench. I inwardly cursed as she smirked and came over to sit next to me, crossing her long stocking-covered legs.

"Evening darling," I grunted a greeting. She stunk of cheap fragrance, and the clothes she wore looked like they were made for somebody twenty years younger. A tight, red T-shirt that stopped just above her navel showed off her slightly saggy stomach, and the red mini she wore showed too much of her scrawny legs. She brushed wrinkled, red nail-varnished fingers through her blonde, dry-looking hair. I didn't know how old she was, but I guessed mid-fifties.

She opened her black handbag and withdrew a cigarette. When she had lit it, she said unto me, "So what are you up to tonight then?"

Even though I didn't want to talk to her, I did. "Ummm... I'm waiting for someone."

The lines around her mouth were exaggerated even more when she drew on her cigarette. "Anyone, I know?"

I shook my head. There were a few minutes of painful silence where I had to try my best not to start coughing on her cigarette smoke. That area of the park was empty, apart from us two. I was about to make a move and leave when the prostitute spoke again. "Listen, mate, have you got anything or what?"

It took a few seconds for me to register what she meant. Drugs, obviously. "No, that's what I'm waiting for. I need to buy some shit."

She laughed out loud and flicked her cigarette-end onto the floor. "Well, you came just at the right time because here come the people you've been waiting for." I didn't know what the hell she was going on about.

I followed her gaze and saw about seven people walking towards us. I was really panicking then. As the group got nearer, I saw that they were all males, and to my surprise, didn't look like what I imagined. A couple of them were wearing normal T-shirt and jeans. There was one chav, and the rest of them looked as though they had been, or were going, clubbing. Smart shirts and trousers.

"Alright, Delia?" Called one of the well-dressed men. The woman beside me got up and went over to the man and kissed him on the cheek. He recoiled in, what I thought was, disgust and said loudly, "Jesus Christ woman, have a Cloret, your breath reeks of cock!" His mates burst into laughter and Delia, the prostitute, cackled with them. She said something to the man and offered him some money. He took it from her and put something in her handbag. As he did this, he noticed me. I saw him look at me, and then turn to Delia. They both turned in my direction. The man beckoned me over.

I reluctantly stood up and went over to him, trying my best not to give the impression that I was petrified. I felt eight sets of eyes on me. "Alright?"

The man smirked at me and mimicked me. "Alright? Delia tells me you're after something? What you after?"

"Err... have you got any 'E's?" I said, a little too quickly. A couple of the other men tittered in the background. The man nodded and patted his trousers' pocket,

"How many do you want? Two for a tenner?"

"Yeah, that'll do for now," I said, wimping out entirely and getting my wallet out. The man fished around in his pocket and withdrew a little plastic bag with some tablets in it. He pulled out two and offered them to me. I gave him a ten-pound note, and he put the tablets in my hand. I muttered a 'Thank you,' and turned to go, cursing myself for my lack of courage.

But then, as the moment almost slipped out of my grasp, I suddenly threw caution to the wind and called out to them. "Hey, hang on a minute!" The whole group turned around and stared at me.

The man, the dealer, took a step towards me. "What?"

So here was the big question. "Have you heard of a guy called 'Skinner'?"

The man frowned, and after a few seconds said, "Yeah, why?"

"I need to talk to you in private," I said, nodding towards the bench. Ok, it wasn't private, but it was away from his cronies. He told his people to stay put and followed me to the bench.

As he sat down, he asked, "What's this about?"

"Are you a friend of Skinner's?" I asked him.

"Well, I'd say I'm a bit more than that." He said vaguely.

"What do you mean?"

"I'm his brother. Look, what's this about? Do you realise my brother's dead?" He suddenly snapped.

"Shit!" I said, wide-eyed. "How?"

"He was in a fight the other week. Some cunt hit him with a hammer! Look, what the hell do you want!?"

My heart pounded in my chest as I said, "I know who committed the murder he was imprisoned for." With that, I took out Stuart's mobile phone and showed him the picture of Jez. "This bloke's name is Jez, and I saw him kill this guy named Stuart."

He took the phone from me and looked at the picture, an expression of pure anger flashed on his face. "I know this bloke. Tell me what happened, everything." He sat there, intently, as I told him how Jez and Stuart had beaten me up that day in the park, and I showed him the photograph of my battered unconscious body lying on the war monument. I spoke the truth, right up until the part where I was following Stuart up the deserted High Street. I said that when he reached McDonald's, I saw another man come up to him, who I recognised as the other bloke who had beaten me up. They seemed to be having an argument, and they started fighting, and that Jez pulled out a knife and attacked him with it.

When Skinner's brother asked me how I had got his phone, I simply said, so I could get revenge on Jez. He took a few minutes to mull over what I had said, then he spoke, "So do you have his address?"

I shook my head, "No, but I've sort of arranged a meeting point for you and him." I told him of the appointed time that Jez was due to be outside The Baker's Oven. He handed the phone back to me and walked off with his friends, and that was the last I saw of Skinner's brother.

I was beginning to think that there must be some sort of divine intervention going on, for everything was just running too smoothly. First of all, I get away with two murders and then get to the point of basically getting someone killed for me, and it was just so easy.

CHAPTER FOURTEEN

Nivek and Kol'n had been arguing a lot since I had asked to join them on their travels. I still had an inkling that Niv still felt something for me, just the way I would catch him looking away quickly when I caught him staring at me. I knew at the time that Kol'n wasn't happy with the fact that I was coming along, so I waited until I caught Niv on his own and confronted him. I think Kol'n was at his parents or something, and for a rare moment, Niv was on his own in the house.

"Niv? Can I ask you something?" I said as soon as I saw he was alone.

He looked up from the book he was reading and said, "You just have!" I detected a hint of annoyance in his tone.

"What's up?"

He just mumbled something and shrugged his shoulders. "Kol'n and I had a disagreement."

I sat down beside him. "It's about me coming travelling with you two next month, isn't it?" For a few seconds, he didn't say anything, and then he slowly nodded.

"He doesn't want you to come with us. It's not that he doesn't like you, it's just that he wants it to be just us."

"Well that's understandable, I mean if I was planning to travel Europe with my girlfriend, or boyfriend, I wouldn't want someone gatecrashing it" As I said this, Niv's face went from the sullen to anger within seconds.

"No, fuck him!!" He shouted. "I've been your friend for a lot longer than I've known him. You're fucking coming!!" I'd never seen Niv so angry before, or since. He threw his book down and stormed off into the adjoining kitchen and started opening and banging some of the cupboard doors. I followed him and watched as he yanked a glass out and slammed it onto the grey-marble work surface. I tried telling him to calm down, but he wouldn't listen. He pulled open the fridge with such force that almost all of the fridge-magnets went flying, and withdrew a bottle of vodka.

"Well if you're having one..." I said, trying to take his mind off being in a foul temper. Niv ripped open the cupboard door again and slammed another glass towards the work surface, but this time it missed and smashed on the tiled floor.

"Oh, fucking hell!" He screamed and crouched down to pick up the pieces of shattered glass. Then suddenly, he burst into tears, and almost instinctively, I knelt down beside him and put my arm around him for comfort. He put his head on my shoulder and wept.

"Come on mate, don't cry. We can sort this out." Was about all I could manage to say. I'm useless in situations like that. Before then, unless it was Seph, if someone cried in the same room as me, I'd freeze, or leave the room. I hugged him, and after at least a minute, he stopped crying. I reached up and grabbed a roll of kitchen-paper and put all the shards of glass into a piece and put them on the counter. I pulled down the remaining glass and the bottle of vodka and filled it. I handed it to Niv, who smiled appreciatively.

Upon seeing that his face was wet with tears, I also handed him a piece of kitchen paper. He took it, but put that and the vodka on the floor. Then he moved his head closer to mine and said, "Thanks, mate," And pressed his lips against mine!! He kissed me!!! I immediately froze. Even though I knew he had a 'thing' for me, I didn't actually believe he would do anything about it. What surprised me, even more, was that I kissed him back! It felt weird kissing Nivek. I felt as though I was watching myself from above. It was as though I had no control over my actions. His lips felt a lot thicker than they appeared, and his breath tasted of Honey and Lemon Lockets. Our tongues entwined, and he bit my lower lip gently. I pushed my tongue into his mouth and flicked it against the piercing he had.

About twenty minutes after that, I had my first sexual encounter with another person. Am I gay? Oh, we didn't have full sex, but we did everything else. (Apart from the term known as 'rimming'.) We were still sat on the kitchen floor when we heard the front door open. Luckily, we were decent and both immediately mimed picking up shards of glass.

Seph walked in, "Hi guys, what are you doing?"

I didn't say, 'We've just kissed and tossed one another off actually. Careful not to slip in that spunk patch beside your right foot!' "Oh," I did say, "Niv, the pisshead, was so desperate for a drink; he smashed a glass, the alcoholic!"

"Clumsy oaf!" Seph tutted and rolled her eyes jokingly and walked across the kitchen. She slipped on… errr… something and I caught her around the waist to stop her from falling. I knew from my reaction that I couldn't be gay. "Fuck's sake, you spill some too?"

Niv and I exchanged a glance, and he bent down with a piece of kitchen paper to wipe the slippery substance off of the floor. "Yeah sorry, missed a bit." I made my excuses and went up to my bedroom contemplating my sexuality. If you'll excuse the pun, I don't know what came over me. Was this a sign that I was gay? I still had strong desires for Seph, but even though I did what I did, I did not have any desires for Nivek. Maybe bi-sexual? I didn't think so because even though I performed these acts with Niv I didn't overly enjoy them. But I didn't entirely dislike them either. And I was obviously aroused at the time. I wasn't appalled by what I had done; I just wished I hadn't had done them. The last thing I wanted was to confuse things for myself. More importantly, I didn't want to fuck things up for Niv or hurt him.

I sat there for so long that I forgot all about the fact that Jez was due to make his appointment and fell asleep and dreamed about an abundance of camp men out of old British sitcoms. John Inman, from Are You Being Served? was the main star, and they all paraded around me chanting, "It's good to be gay!"

So yeah, the next time I thought about Jez and his appointment was the next evening, when I purchased a local paper on my way home from work. Things had gone slightly worse than I had intended. The newspaper headline read: 'IPSWICH FAMILY GUNNED DOWN IN DRIVE-BY SHOOTING!' Below this was a photograph of Jez, a woman, and a little brown-haired boy of five. I was responsible for the murders of two innocent people. That was a lot to take in. My bedroom door stayed closed for the rest of the day as I wept, as quietly as I could, over the face of the five-year-old boy whose face haunted me—and still does each and every time I close my eyes. I am an evil, warm-blooded killer.

CHAPTER FIFTEEN

Following the shock of Jez and his family's murder, I hardly spoke to anyone in the house at all. I refused to tell anyone what was the matter. As if I could even start to explain! Niv was acting even weirder than ever and somehow got it into his head that the reason I was so withdrawn was because of our little experience. He had been seeing Kol'n even more now that the trip was almost planned. I had managed to persuade him that I would stay with them for a couple of days when we first crossed the channel and travelled into Belgium, but then we would go our separate ways. But as I said, he was still paranoid that my silence was due to him. In the end, I just had to sit him down and speak to him about the ordeal and also confess something else.

I explained much to his disappointment, that I only loved him as a friend and I could not fathom why I had acted the way I did when he kissed me. I did tell him that I knew he had feelings for me, and I knew he came into my bedroom that night. At first, he was mortified at this revelation, but I assured him that I was flattered then and was now. I apologised as much as I could about the thing we did. He told me that he was happy with Kol'n, and the only reason Kol'n was being arsey about the whole Europe-thing was because of the fact that he knew of Niv's feelings toward me. So that was when I decided to go off on my own, and I agreed to stay in touch with them and we would meet up at some point, somewhere.

I also told him, in the strictest confidence, of my feelings towards Seph, and he shocked me by saying that he knew already, that I couldn't be more blatant if I tried!

Something else happened before we went that made me feel even guiltier for leaving Seph and Thys hunting for future housemates. Thys's father, who, as you know, originates from Italy, was given a proposal he could not refuse. He was offered a ridiculous amount of money to move to Italy for a year to start up another chain of the virtually-global insurance company he worked for. Thys's mother and he would be joining them, as he had shown great potential and interest in following in his father's footsteps. I was pleased for him, although slightly peeved at the waste of four years at Art College if he was going to work for his father.

His father insisted that he would pay for six months' rent of the house that we stayed in to allow Seph time to find suitable housemates, she reluctantly agreed, even though I could tell she didn't like the prospect of interviewing loads of unknowns for three bedrooms. Her look when she realised that she was going to be the last one left there broke my heart. How could I leave her? But I knew that I must. I could not stay in the country much longer, for I knew that sooner or later, the guilt over the child's death would become too much, and I would've given myself up. I HAD to leave Seph and England. However, even though I was running away from England, work and Seph, the true person I needed to run away from was myself.

There were a couple more ups and downs before I left the country. I worked at the supermarket right up until the night before we left for Holland. This was mostly for the money, and so I wouldn't have to endure any prolonged, 'goodbyes' with Seph. I had noticed she had been acting really down leading up to our departure, and even though I expected tears, I knew it would be one of the hardest things for me to do.

The people at work knew that I was going travelling around Europe. Niv's mum obviously knew, although I never actually witnessed him contact her. Of course, there were loads of comments made about us three 'gays' going off 'camping' etc. On my last night, I really tried to avoid everyone and just keep to myself, more than usual. It was a weird atmosphere in the shop on my last day, quiet, no one was nasty to me, they either just didn't say anything or showed interest in my travels. Usually, as the supermarket workers all had to work late, as it was their bi-annually stock take, the workers would be pissed off over the fact that they'd be working till 10 pm. I thought they would be arsey with me, seeing as I was getting out 2 hours earlier than the rest of them. I did feel slightly paranoid, but I honestly thought they had just given up on the torment purely because I was leaving.

I was especially taken aback when nearing the end of my final shift, Steve, the most fancied man in the shop, came up to me, all smiles, and said, "Hey dude, I know this is your last shift, and your setting sail tomorrow, so a few of us got together and got you something for your travels." I was extremely dubious but decided to play along.

As it was time to finish, we, well he, made idle chitchat about going out the previous night and meeting a girl, who was half his age, and getting her phone number and described his intentions towards her. I didn't comment much, but just got my stuff and continued to the exit. He kept by my side until we left the back of the building. When I got outside, I realised he had been taking the piss. There were about five of the twatty male workers who hung around Niv's mum and standing with them, her face a mask of maliciousness, Niv's mum looked at me as if I was the filthiest piece of shit she had ever set eyes upon. She took one last drag on the cigarette she was smoking and flicked the butt at me.

I stared in pure hatred at her and said, "Fuck you!" and went to walk around them and leave. Steve and two of the other blokes grabbed me and held me still against the shop wall. I attempted to struggle but gave up almost immediately, it was a waste of strength, and I couldn't get away. One of the other men got a metal stock cage and wheeled it over to where I was. I was then manhandled into the cage and I let them shut it on me. I was yelling out, but I don't think anyone would care. I just stood in the cage, wondering what was going to happen next. I knew this wasn't just some joke they played on leavers. They all looked too sinister. I felt like Edward Woodward in The Wicker Man, being tricked into being captured with no possibility of getting away.

One of the men approached the cage with a huge roll of polythene wrap that the warehouse used to wrap the filled cages when sending stock out. Oh fuck, I thought, they're going to stick me in one of the lorries or something! The man started wrapping the cage, ignoring my protests. In the end, I just shut up and let them do what they felt like they had to. I constantly stared at Steve and Niv's Mum. Even though the film on the cage warped my view slightly, I could see that the evil expressions on their faces were the same.

I saw someone wheeling something over towards me. It took a few seconds for me to register what it was, and then it hit me. I could tell by the bright green colour, it was the wheelie bin that the greengrocery section put all the damaged and rotten vegetables and fruit in. It was usually only emptied once a month, and I knew for a fact it'd be nigh on full. I knew what they were going to do. It took all of the men to lift the full bin and rest the edge of it on the open top of the cage. I now understood why they wrapped the cage. I braced myself as the stench of putrid liquefied rotten vegetables hit me.

I put my hands over my face as they poured the contents of the whole bin on top of me. Oh, Jesus, it was foul. Some of the stuff in there was warm and squishy, other stuff was cold and slimy. I started retching as the stuff covered me all over. I tried to take a breath and got a mouthful of brown juice that caused me to be sick. The vomit added to the stench around and on me. And once I'd started vomiting, I couldn't stop. I was drenched. The actual contents of the bin came up to my chest. I could see some of it slowly leaking out of the base of the cage. I couldn't see through the film now, as it was covered, like me, in the brown sludge. I heard the cackles and laughter though.

Then I heard someone open the back of the shop and call that the manager was coming down. I listened to the seven of them go back inside, sniggering. As soon as they had left, I tried to get out of the cage. Climbing out was too difficult, as everything was too slippery, so I started rocking the thing back and forth, until it rolled across the ground, hit an uneven piece, and eventually toppled over. It fucking hurt when it fell over, and I was shortly covered from head to toe in sludge. It was a harrowing ordeal, and when I crawled from the top of the cage, I burst into tears. I burst into tears, but at the same time, felt a hatred inside of me that was so intense I felt as though it would rip itself out of me and unleash itself upon the nearest person. I trudged homewards stinking like a fucker.

Miraculously, my mobile phone survived the incident, and I automatically turned to the first person I turn to in times of crisis. Seph. She seemed so pleased to hear from me like we hadn't spoken in ages. Well, even though we lived in the same house, we hadn't, what with my trying to avoid her and all. I told her what had happened, and that I could not enter the house as filthy as I was. I was soaked right through.

I walked through town in a trance-like state and arrived at our house. I went around to the back-door of the house and rang Seph to tell her I was there. She came to the door with a disgusted, but sympathetic look on her face. Bless her; she had laid a trail of newspaper from the back-door to the bathroom, which I followed, muttering an appreciative 'Thank you' along the way. The whole bathroom floor was covered in newspaper and the window wide open.

"Chuck anything that is not good out of the window," Seph called to me through the door. I did as she told me to. I had to throw everything I was wearing out of there, even my shoes. The contents of my bag were fine, but the bag itself was not. I threw all the crappy stuff that was mainly my work uniform, so not actually mine, out of the window and got into the hot bath that Seph had prepared for me, nestled down into the suds, and shut my eyes. I had enough. That was going to be my last night in England! Images swirled and faded inside my head like a kaleidoscope, depicting different ways and means of inflicting harm upon Niv's Mum and Steve.

I felt a strange alien smile slither across my face as a little voice chirruped in my head, "One for the road?"

CHAPTER SIXTEEN

I came out of the bath a different man. It was as if the warm, soapy water had baptised me and had traversed my conscious mind to another state. Everything was crystal clear to me; I put on the clean clothes that Seph had sat on the toilet for me with almost no recollection. As soon as I had washed, I left the house quickly, before Seph had a chance to speak to me.

Within half an hour, I was back outside the rear of the supermarket. It was just getting dark, the night clouds were on the horizon, and there was a strange metallic spark to add to the chilliness of the dusk air. I sat half-hidden amongst some bales of flattened cardboard boxes that sat opposite the exit. The baler had just been emptied, as it is every week. It used to be one of my duties, taking out the cardboard boxes that the women couldn't be arsed to flatten. I loved doing it, getting away from them, loading the baler, and watching as the huge weight crushed the boxes I'd laid in there. It was a colossal piece of equipment and took up a large percentage of the yard at the back.

I sat beside it, picking at the flaking, green paint that adorned its fast-rusting surface. It felt like a few seconds that I had been sitting there before the exit door opened, but it wasn't.

As luck would have it, Niv's Mum came out first, on her own. Thinking back, I would have preferred her to have come out last, but at the time, I was calm and relaxed. I watched as she lit up a cigarette and I thought that I'd better do it now before someone else comes out. I strolled, coolly, towards her with something of a grin on my face.

She jumped when she saw me, muttered something under her breath, and carried on puffing away on her smoke. She was obviously waiting for someone. Nevertheless, I moved around behind her, as if to go in the exit door. In one swift motion, I slipped my right arm around her neck and clamped my hand over her mouth—burning my palm on her fag in the process. She put up a tremendous struggle, so I tightened my arm against her throat and whispered in her ear, "Do as I say, or I'll really hurt you!"

I half-dragged her to the side of the supermarket where there was a narrow path that ran the length of the building. I pushed her up against the fence that ran parallel to the path and risked taking a hand off her face. She attempted a scream, but I slapped her across the face and told her politely to 'shut up'. She looked at me with fear in her crow's feet-framed eyes.

"Are you going to rape me?" It made my stomach churn just to picture it. However...

"Yes, but first I'm going to kill you!" I'm sure, for a flicker of a millisecond, I saw a frown wrinkle her already-wrinkled forehead when I said that. Then the realisation that I said I was 'going to kill her' sunk in and she screamed and tried to get away from me. I grabbed her by the arm and swung her into the wall. There was a sickening crunch as her head struck brick. She clutched her head and groggily lashed out at me, almost raking her long nails against my cheek. I punched her fully in the face, and she fell to the ground.

Wasting no time, I knelt to the side of her, fastened my hands around her neck, and squeezed as hard as I could. Her eyes bulged, and spittle formed on her lips. She tried to pull my hands away from her throat. The stench of cigarettes was overwhelming, being this close to her. She started to make a gargling noise, and finally, I felt her go weak, and her hands flopped down to her sides. I let go of her throat and was going to feel for a pulse, but I was annoyingly interrupted by a blow to the head.

I don't know how long I was unconscious; it could've only been a couple of seconds. I came round to find that I was lying next to Niv's Mum on my belly. Someone was crouching over her, attempting to resuscitate her. I recognised the trendy hair-do to be that of Steve. As soon as he saw I had come to, he shouted, "I saw you! You've fucking killed her!"

I stood up slowly. "Oh my God what have I done?" I covered my face with my hands.

"I always knew you were a fucking nutter!" Steve said as he tried once more to resuscitate Niv's Mum. He shook his head and started to get up, and as he turned to face me, my boot connected with his jaw. He toppled back and fell on the dead body of Niv's mum. Before he had a chance to get to his feet, I leapt onto him, landing knee-first onto his stomach, winding him. He clutched at my sides and tried to move me, but my weight was on my side. I threw a few punches at his face, splitting his lip and breaking his nose. I pushed my hand into his mouth, to stop him from making a noise, but he bit me hard. I yelped, took my hand away from his mouth and hit him again.

I started to panic, Steve was a lot stronger than Niv's Mum, and I didn't know whether I could hold him for much longer. In the struggle, I had allowed myself to slide down his body somewhat and put myself in a foolishly vulnerable position, to which he took advantage of. His knee went up and into my groin hard. I rolled up in pain, and he pushed me off of him. Steve got to his feet immediately and was about to run when Niv's Mum's handbag stopped him. His foot got tangled in the strap where it lay, and he tripped, falling flat on his face.

Despite the pain I was going through, I knelt on his back and grabbed him by the hair. I put one hand on his forehead and one below his chin and pulled his head back as far as I could. I could hear him straining as I forced his head back into an angle that it wasn't capable of making. Finally, something snapped and Steve was still, and I breathed a well-earned sigh of relief.

I sat for a few minutes, on the bodies of Steve and Niv's Mum, catching my breath. Upon checking my watch, I saw that it was twenty past ten. The exit door opened about seven times as other workers left. I waited until I didn't think there would be any more people coming out and snuck around to the exit to see if the place was empty. I looked through the small hatch in the delivery door, and all was dark. Only the security light remained on.

I went back to the side, looked at the dark shapes of the two fresh corpses and tutted, and wondered what the fuck I was going to do with them. Then the moon came out from behind a cloud, as if giving some sign, and shone a beam down upon the flaky, green paint of the cardboard box baler. An imaginary light-bulb pinged on above my head as I had an idea.

CHAPTER SEVENTEEN

Once I had the cardboard-box baler loaded, I made my way back to the house. Even though I was as sore as hell, I had no visible signs of conflict. When I got back, I entered the living-room to see that everyone was there. Niv and Kol'n sat side by side on the sofa, Seph lounged in an armchair, and Thys sat in the other chair with a young attractive blonde perched on the arm. I found I could barely look Niv in the eye, not out of guilt, but some other emotion unknown to me.

Seph looked up questioningly as if to ask of my disappearance. I sat on the arm of her chair.

"Thought I'd go back and make an official complaint about those idiots' prank." I lied to them all.

"What did your twat of an ex-manager say?" Seph said coldly.

"Fuck all." I said to a chorus of 'bastards'.

I made a subtle eye-gesture in the direction of Thys's blonde. Thys smiled and said, "Tabby, this is God. God this is Tabby." I nodded and grinned a greeting and winked at Thys.

Looking around, I said, "So which one of you is going to get me a beer? Seeing as you've all got one!"

"Huh, you can get one yourself, seeing as you're deserting me tomorrow!" Seph said, half-joking. I tutted and walked the long trek into the kitchen. We sat and chatted with one another, and despite the new faces, it was like the good old times again, before all the shit began.

Thys's blonde, Tabby, was his date for the evening. Without my realising, he had become quite a lady-killer, and apparently, Tabby had been his sixth conquest in a month. He was the first to leave, and before I saw him for the last time, he produced three small packages from behind his chair and distributed them to me, Niv, and Kol'n. I unwrapped the small, square parcel and found a black box inside. Inside the black box was a small silver flask with 'Robert Goddard', engraved upon it. I was delighted to find that it was full. I was really touched by this, as were Niv and Kol'n who had identical gifts.

He hugged us all goodbye and told us that he would see us in just over a year if we were back by then. Then he left taking Tabby, who hadn't even uttered a word, just smiled prettily, and that was the last I saw of him.

It was horrible watching Thys go and knowing that I would probably never see him again. Each time I looked at Seph that evening, I could see tears in her eyes. I felt unbelievably guilty about leaving her in the house on her own and could see that was probably why she was upset.

The two guys and I finalised wake-up times and everything and stuck all our luggage downstairs, ready to leave in the morning. Niv and Kol'n said a tearful 'goodbye' to Seph, even though she promised to wave us farewell in the morning, and went to bed.

That left Seph and me alone together. There was an uncomfortable atmosphere about us that I'd never experienced around her. We sat in virtual silence; every now and then we'd ask one another a question that we'd answer in as few words as possible. Then I just came out with it. "Oh Jesus, I'm so sorry about leaving!"

She frowned. "What are you on about?"

"I feel so guilty. For leaving you on your own to sort things out around here." I said, tears welling up in my eyes.

She sat forward and placed her bottle on the coffee table. "Don't be stupid. I'll sort it out!" she said, reassuringly.

"Oh come on, I know you've been pissed off about this whole thing." I sighed. "There's no point in denying it."

"Look, I'm not pissed off about you all leaving. It's just that I've been preparing myself to have all my closest friends leave me. I'm going to miss you!" Seph leant forward and hugged me. "I've got used to having you guys around, that's all." I melted into her arms, feeling her that close made me question leaving once again. As politely as I could, I eased myself away from her, I hoped, without her noticing.

"I'll miss you too, but you know it's not going to be that long. You know me; I'll be back within a few months! And as for postcards, you won't be able to move for postcards!" I looked at her beautiful, smiling face and could see a few tears nestling on her cheeks. When I wiped them away with my thumbs, neither of us was shocked at such an intimate gesture; I ached so much to kiss her. We sat back on the couch, neither of us eager to go to bed, chatted and reminisced for possibly the last time.

The following morning came, and after a much-rushed, 'goodbye' we got into the taxi and set off on the hour's drive to the port of Harwich. Nothing really much happened during our two-hour wait at the port or throughout our four and a half hour journey across the water to the Hook of Holland. We mostly just found somewhere to sleep.

I didn't think that the further away I got from Seph would make it any easier, but I also didn't realise how much it would hurt. It was as though I had torn something inside my chest. It hurt to breathe, and it drenched all the guilt I had been feeling about the slaughter I had partaken in.

As England disappeared from view, I almost had a premonition of what was to unfold. The white, frothy sea, left by the ferry's passage, reminded me of aspirins dissolving in water. It gave me an idea, one that I had not, at first, considered. Some other way to ease the pain of my shredded heart strands. Another way to, 'start again'.

We arrived, mid-afternoon, at the Hook of Holland and got a bus to Zeebrugge. Niv and Kol'n chatted mostly amongst themselves, as I pretended to be more tired than I was so I could fake sleep. I desperately wanted to be alone, to dwell in self-pity, guilt, and my Seph-sickness.

Now and again, I opened my eyes to glimpse snippets of Zeebrugge, but all I saw of it was through tired-eyes, below dull grey cold skies, and the constant drizzle of rain. Mostly, it was industrial; huge factories expelled thick, white plumes of smoke into the already bleak clouds. The weather would've probably been much the same when my idol, Alex Harvey, had died here back in '82. I imagined dying then, and the last image that flitted before my eyes would have been the ghastly-grey and brown factory looming monstrously through a dirty, Belgium bus window.

Apparently, Alex Harvey had two heart attacks: One at the Zeebrugge port whilst waiting to return to England, I think it would have been Kingston-Upon-Hull, and the other in one of Zeebrugge's hospitals. I didn't want to visit the port and neither the hospital. I just wanted to see what the place looked like for myself. We finally got to Zeebrugge and got off at the stop that the driver insisted was where our guesthouse was. After much swearing, map reading, and getting drenched, we found a shabby, three-storey detached house in a solemn street that was lined with cheap-looking bars and takeaways.

A weather-battered sign squeaked on rusted hooks. In plain gold letters, the sign told us that this was, in fact, our lodgings. I picked it purely on the name. Translated, it means: 'The Rising Sun'. The Rising Sun is the name of a really cool pub that another mate of mine, called Dave Smith, frequents with his mate Ian Maiden in Walsall. I've visited it a few times, an excellent pub.

I knocked on the door, and after a few seconds, someone answered. A middle-aged man wearing a white shirt and the trousers and waistcoat of a three-piece, tweed suit answered the door. A paisley handkerchief was tied around his neck. He had an incredibly bad comb-over hairstyle and a concerned look on his face. I introduced myself and told him who we were and what we were there for, and he allowed us in. I don't know whether it was because his English wasn't very good, or he was being ignorant, but he hardly spoke to us. He only said his name was Jakob.

The place, to be honest, was nasty. It didn't look as though it had been decorated since the seventies, and almost everything was either orange or brown. However, we found that although everything looked old and the furniture, cheap, it was relatively clean. He showed us to our rooms, told us what time breakfast was and left us to it.

On our way into the guesthouse, I noticed a bar on the other side of the road called The Boathouse, with a big neon sign that flickered, 'karaoke'. And I thought, "Hmmm that looks interesting."

CHAPTER EIGHTEEN

By the time we had settled into our rooms, it was getting on early evening. We each had separate rooms, and I had been lying on the bed beginning this confessional/autobiography for about an hour and a half before a knock came on the door. I stuffed this notebook beneath one of the pillows and opened the door. It was the owner of the guesthouse.

"Err, sorry to disturb you..." He said, in his strange accent, and never looking me in the eye. He was sweating profusely, and the strands that attempted to cover his bald-head glistened with it. "I forget to tell you previously. You must, if you go out late at night, be quiet when you arrive back here. My father, he is very ill, and I do not want him disturbed."

"That's fine, if we go out, we won't be back that late, and we'll make sure to keep it down," I said with a grin. As I spoke to him, he turned his ear towards me and had a serious look of concentration on his face. I don't know whether he fully understood what I said, but he smiled, showing crooked, yellowy-brown teeth, turned, and walked off with one hand pressed against his lower back.

No sooner had I shut the door, than another knock came at the door. I opened it, expecting Jakob to tell me something else that I shouldn't do because of his father. It was Niv and Kol'n. I let them in and they slumped down on my bed.

"So, are we going out now or what?" Niv asked me as if I was the leader of our trio. I nodded and told them to give me five minutes whilst I got ready.

I pulled a clean shirt out of my bag and went into the miniscule bathroom. I took the elastic band from my hair and ran a comb through it to stop it looking like the mess it was. The black-stripes that I used to top up so regularly were fading fast. I needed to shave, but I couldn't be arsed, so I made a decision there and then to grow a beard. Besides, it would be considerably cheaper than having to buy shaving stuff. I splashed some water on my face and sprayed myself with deodorant.

I came out of the bathroom and we left. As we walked across the brown-carpeted landing, we heard shouting coming from the top of the stairway to the third floor. At the bottom of the stairs, a red rope with a sign reading, 'Private' acted as a banner. We stood, in silence, and heard what sounded like Jakob saying in a quiet pleading tone, "Yes Pappa, I will tell them." And then all of a sudden, we heard him cry out, "No Pappa, please don't do that!"

We looked at one another, unsure what to do, not understanding anything the man was saying. As we carried on, we heard a deep, fierce voice shout, "Stop, idiot child. Get my dinner now!" And then we heard the door open up the stairs.

We hurried out of the guesthouse.

We headed straight for The Boathouse bar on my decision and mainly because of the rain that was pissing down in torrents. The bar was surprisingly familiar; it had all the furnishings of a traditional, English pub. There were few people all sitting alone, nursing glasses of beer, lager, and shots of spirits. We marched up to the bar, where a portly man with a huge handlebar-moustache stood; arms folded watching a television set that was mounted on a wall in the corner.

He looked at us and said something foreign. I didn't know what the hell that meant, but I took it that he was asking us what we wanted. I really didn't want to do that thing that all English do when they're abroad and shout English words as if the other person would understand. Instead, I spoke clearly and hoped that the man could understand English.

"Hello, could I...," I pointed to myself, "Please have two..," I put two fingers up, "...bottles of..," I scanned the array of beers and saw one that was amusingly called Bush, "...Bush beer and a vodka and coke please?"

The portly man looked at us for a second, and then said, "Yeah, course you can mate is Pepsi alright?" In an Australian accent.

I chuckled, "I'm glad I didn't try my Dutch out now!"

The barman laughed. "Oh you should have, I could've done with a laugh. So why the hell have you kids decided to come to bloody Zeebrugge?"

"Ahh well, it's our first stop off point. We're doing the obligatory student-thing and backpacking Europe." Niv said watching as the barman poured a rather large measure of vodka into a glass.

"Excellent!" The barman said as he filled the glass with Pepsi. "That's how I ended up here! But this was my last stop before I went to England."

"What made you stay?" I asked.

The barman laughed and said, "I often ask myself that same question! Nah, I guess the place has some kind of charm, well it did back then. I met a girl over here back in the seventies, and we got married and bought this place." his eyes seemed to well up with some fond memory. "But the bitch went off and shagged someone half her fucking age three years ago and left me."

"Shit, I'm sorry to hear that," I said, watching as he bent down to get two bottles of Bush out.

"I ain't," He said, placing the bottles next to the vodka and coke. "I've done exactly the same; got myself a fiancée who's twenty now! And I have a lot more fun than I ever did with my bloody wife, I can tell you!" He roared with laughter and took the money that Kol'n offered him. "So are you kids going to stay for the karaoke? Starts in an hour."

"Yeah, why not," I said taking my bottle.

"Excellent, if you're lucky, I'll do my Tom Jones. So, you staying at Jake's place?" he asked, addressing Kol'n.

"Well, that depends if 'Jake' is the owner of The Rising Sun?" Kol'n answered.

The barman nodded. "Yeah, that's Jake's place alright. What a bloody fruitcake!"

We must've looked concerned because the barman grinned mischievously. "Have you met his father yet?"

I shook my head. "We only arrived this afternoon. We did hear some shouting earlier though."

"Ah, that'll be his dad shouting at him alright. Let you into a little secret though." He leant across the bar and lowered his voice. "His dad's been dead for fifteen years!"

"What the fuck?" Niv spluttered wide-eyed.

"Yeah," The barman continued, "Apparently, his old man fell down the stairs and broke his neck. Jake used to hate his old man. His dad used to be a wrestler back in the sixties, a massive,

massive bloke he was. And even when he got old and frail, he was still huge and strong. But his mind went, and Jake, whose mum died when he was five, had to look after his dad. His dad had a really violent temper and would take his anger out on Jake when he was a kid. When his dad went funny in the head, Jake and his wife, he was married then, they ran the guesthouse; she agreed to let his dad move in. It was a disaster from the word go; his dad used to expose himself to Jake's wife, and because he was confused all the time, he'd get angry and hit Jake again. He used to come in here black and blue sometimes." The barman stared off into the reminiscence of Jakob's past.

"So what happened?" I asked, slightly concerned that we were staying with a potential nutter.

The barman continued, "Well, one day, his wife and his dad were in the house on their own, and his dad forces himself onto Jake's wife and... you know..."

"Fuck! He raped her!" Niv exclaimed.

The barman nodded. "His wife left there and then and stayed with her family. Jake was distraught; he could not afford to put his dad away anywhere. He didn't tell the authorities about what his dad did, and neither did his wife. Eventually, she divorced Jake and found another man. Jake spent all his time running the guesthouse, not that he got many customers mind, and looking after his dad. The worse his dad got, the worse he would beat Jake. As he got older, he needed a walking stick, and this was often used on Jake. Then one day, his dad got so worked up that he really beat the shit out of Jake, and his dad pushed him down the stairs, and as Jake fell, he grabbed hold of his old man's stick. His dad lost his balance and came tumbling down with him. Jake fell so hard, he was knocked out, and when he came round, his dad was lying across him, dead."

We just sat there shocked by this story.

"Jake sat there for three days with his father before calling the ambulance to take him away. Jake has never been right since. Still insists his father is alive and living with him. He doesn't come in here anymore, but one of the last times he came in here, he was covered in bruises, and when I asked him what had happened, he told me he had an argument with his dad! This was five years after he had died!"

I was flabbergasted. I didn't know what to say, but I did, however, want to be out of that guesthouse immediately. I couldn't believe we were staying with Belgium's answer to Norman Bates!

CHAPTER NINETEEN

With the ominous thoughts of the tragedy of Jakob playing on our minds and taking up most of our conversation, we went to sit at a table and wait for the food we had ordered with Boyd the barman.

"I think we should leave the guesthouse immediately!" Niv said, worriedly.

Kol'n looked at him foolishly. "Don't worry about it, the guy seems okay."

"Yeah," I added, "Besides there's no reason to believe he's a violent nutter. I really feel sorry for him; think about how much that man has lost. We're only staying here a few days. Relax, Niv mate."

Niv moved a strand of his long, black hair from his vodka and coke and sighed. "I suppose so, but I'm sharing my room with you!" He said, looking at Kol'n.

"Fair enough." Kol'n said with a wink.

Our food was delivered by a young, curvaceous blonde girl who wore a smart little, black skirt and a white blouse. As I was the only heterosexual person at the table, I alone admired her shapely figure. Boyd caught my eye from the bar, winked and called out, "Hey, stop eyeing up my fiancée!"

By the time we had finished our meals, the place had filled up with people of all ages. Boyd had set up the karaoke machine, stood on the small stage, and spoke into the microphone. "Right who's first?" There were a few mumbles, but no one seemed eager to step up. I don't think anyone was drunk enough to make a fool of themselves. Boyd cleared his throat. "Oh come on. Tell you what, whoever comes up here and sings a song, gets a free drink."

As soon as he'd said that, a man went up to the stage and started browsing through the song lists. And as the man chose his song and launched into a deafening rendition of Shirley Bassey's, 'Hey Big Spender' I got another round of Bush beers in. We had really taken a liking to this strange, Belgium beer. It was 12% and tasted like it had whiskey in it. After I had taken the bottles to the table, I had a browse in the song-list book, just out of curiosity to see what songs they had on offer.

As I flicked through the laminated pages, I was amazed to actually see some decent songs listed alongside the karaoke regulars. A few Black Sabbath, a couple of Led Zeppelin, and even one Nick Cave! I was almost tempted to go up and sing one. But as I decided not to bother, I noticed and Alex Harvey song on there, 'Boston Tea Party'. I decided that seeing as I was in a foreign country and everything; I would have a few more drinks and do it. I would sing an Alex Harvey song in the town where he died! It would be a tribute to the great man.

"Are you going to the party? Are you going to the Boston Tea Party?" I spoke the first two lines of the SAHB song and looked blurry-eyed at the audience. A few whistles and cheers came from Niv and Kol'n as I began the song. I just hoped I wasn't too pissed not to do the song justice."

"And that's the reason you all Americans drink coffee." I began by reading the lyrics off the small monitor, but the words were about a second behind. So, as I knew the song by heart anyway, I just ignored the monitor and continued with the singing.

"Are you going to the party? Are you going to the Boston Tea Party?" By the time I had finished, I was feeling really drunk and stumbled off the stage to the applause that was coming from Niv and Kol'n. I slumped in my chair and noticed the big, bulky figure of Boyd towering over me, three Bush beers in his hands.

"Fantastic mate, Alex Harvey eh? Great, here are your free drinks."

He handed me my drink, which I just managed to grasp and turned to the other two and said, "Your turn now." Niv and

Kol'n looked at one another, Niv shaking his head, Kol'n grinning and nodding his.

Kol'n led Niv up to the stage and started going through the song list. Just before I fell into a drunken slumber, I heard the start of Niv and Kol'n singing 'Something's Gotten Hold of My Heart' by Gene Pitney. I think they were attempting the Marc Almond/Gene Pitney version. Niv, I think, was being Marc Almond. But unfortunately, I fell asleep spilling three-quarters of a bottle of Bush over myself.

When I awoke, Niv and Kol'n were standing over me. They helped me up, and together, we said farewell to Boyd and his lovely fiancée and left the bar. The thing that annoys me when I'm drunk is that even when I try to be quiet, I'm far too loud, and we were shamefully loud when we got back to The Rising Sun. I dropped the keys about three times, and we were all 'Shhh-ing' one another excessively noisily.

We finally got into the house and managed to get to our rooms in virtual silence. Kol'n got me into my room, and I fell onto the bed in a comatose heap.

Somehow, I made it down to breakfast without the hangover I was expecting. I sat in the orange sitting room alone, whilst Jakob pottered about, bringing big, silver pots of tea and coffee, whilst I helped myself to the small array of rolls, sliced meats, and cheeses. He never mentioned anything about us being noisy the previous night, so I was relieved we didn't wake him, or his 'dad'.

Kol'n came marching into the sitting room, smiled at Jakob, and said, "Good morning, are you and your father well?"

He grinned awkwardly and muttered, "Yes, we are both fine." And disappeared into the kitchen.

"Is Niv up?" I asked Kol'n, whilst buttering a roll. When he never answered, I looked up from my roll. Kol'n's face was like thunder. "What's wrong mate?" I asked worrying slightly.

He looked at me and in five words, managed to chill me to the very core. "I read your notebook!"

I put the roll down. "Oh right, and what did you think?"

"What the fuck do you expect me to think? It is true, isn't it?" Kol'n said, calmly but coldly.

I thought for a while before I answered his question. I thought about what he might do if I said 'yes' and what he'd do if I said 'no'. I thought of how much I had written. I think I had just finished my encounter with Atkins. Theoretically, two murders, well if you can count Atkins. I decided to be honest with him. I was fucked either way. I was about to answer when there came a bloodcurdling scream from upstairs.

Jakob rushed through the room shouting, "No Pappa, stop!" and ran towards the stairs. I jumped up, grabbed one of the heavy, metal coffee pots and brought it down as hard as I could across the back of Kol'n's head. He crashed to the floor and lay still. I ran up the stairs, two at a time, and across the landing. I could see down the hallway that Niv's door was open. Angry shouts in Dutch came from the room as I approached. I could hear Jakob pleading, could hear Niv crying out in pain, but worst of all, I could hear the chilling voice of Jakob's dad!

I had visions of Jakob attacking Niv and putting on the two voices like the fucking nutter that he evidently was. But as I turned and looked across the threshold, I saw one of the most horrific sights I had ever seen. Then I remembered that the scream we heard had come before Jakob had gone upstairs.

Like I said, the sight before me was so terrifying, so petrifying, that for several seconds, I froze, rooted to the spot, unable to comprehend what I was actually seeing.

CHAPTER TWENTY

Nivek was naked, pinned to the bed by hands the size of bear-paws. A huge man, who looked in his seventies, but could have been older, lay on top of him, one of his big hands pushing Nivek's face into the pillows, the other holding both of his thin arms behind his back. The giant man wore a dressing gown, it was hanging open, and he made animal-like grunts as he raped Nivek. Jakob lay on the floor beside a broken walking stick; a severe red mark ran across his forehead. He didn't move at all, I would later find out that he was dead.

Boyd had obviously been lying when he told us the tale of Jacob's dad, as this person could be no other. I launched myself at him, screaming and raining blows down upon his big head. He struck out a fist, which hit me square in the face and sent me reeling. I fell down next to Jakob, amazed by the old man's strength. I picked up the longest end of the broken walking stick and started beating the man about the head with it. It seemed to have no effect at all. He struck out again, and I felt my lip split as I collided with the doorpost.

I went crazy and ran to the bed, lifted the walking stick high above my head, and jumped up and brought the sharp, broken end of the stick down into the old man's back. It went into him about a couple of inches, and he let out a bloodcurdling yell and climbed off Nivek. He stumbled towards me, dressing gown hanging open, revealing his sagging, naked body, and his prominent erection to me. In a fit of rage, he lunged for me, but as he was obviously bad on his legs, he couldn't move very quickly. I backed into the hallway as Jakob's father hurled, what I supposed was Dutch abuse at me. I walked back slowly, I didn't want the old man to go back to the room and finish what he was doing to Niv. I stood at the top of the stairs and watched as the old man shuffled as quickly as he could along the hallway, his hands pressed against the walls for support.

As he got nearer, I started down the stairs. The old man stopped at the top of the stairs, and suddenly, the expression of pure rage changed into one of despair as he took the first step with much difficulty. The frightened look on his face almost made me pity him. He got to the third step down, and the inevitable happened: He lost his footing and fell forwards. I jumped out of the way as he came thundering down the stairs.

I don't know whether Boyd was psychic, or what, but as soon as I heard the loud crack when the old man hit the floor, I knew what happened. His neck broke. I ran back up the stairs, my heart drumming in my chest. My heart broke when I went into Niv's bedroom. Niv lay on his front, face still half-buried in the pillow. The skin on his face was a bluish-purple colour. I knelt on the bed beside him and felt for a pulse. There was none. Red marks and scratches bled all over his back and buttocks. I tried to perform first aid on him, but it was no good.

Niv was dead.

I went downstairs and lifted the still unconscious body of Kol'n up and restrained him in my bedroom. I dragged the bodies of Jakob and his father down to the basement beneath the stairs. Only after, did I go back into Nivek's room, fully dressed his dead body, sat there, and wept for at least three hours. It was early afternoon by the time I wrapped Nivek's body in the bed sheet and went into my room.

I had tied Kol'n to the sturdiest chair I could find with a couple of belts and gagged him with a pair of socks. When I went into my room, he sat on the chair wide-eyed and frightened. I sat opposite him and opened the full bottle of whiskey I had found in one of Jakob's cupboards. I told him to listen, and over the following hour, I told him everything that had happened, every little detail of my crimes. He wept when I told him of Nivek's murder, and I joined him.

After a while, I took the gag off and gave him some of the whiskey. He kept pleading with me to let him go, that he wouldn't tell anyone. I didn't know what to do. In the end, I just gagged him again, cleaned myself up, and left the guesthouse to get some air. The cold rain that seemed to have been constant ever since we arrived sobered me up and soaked me through. I was lost, my best friend was dead, and I didn't know what I was going to do.

Whilst I wandered, I bought more alcohol and enough food for me and Kol'n for a few days. I ignored Boyd when I walked past him as he opened up The Boathouse. I arrived back at the guesthouse, fed Kol'n, sat cross-legged on the bed, and wrote this letter to Seph:

Dear Seph,

I don't know how to start this, but I may as well just come straight to the point. I am a mass-murderer! This is not a joke; believe me, I wish it were. It started with your Stuart. On that night so long ago, when I caught you kissing, I followed him through town listening to the vile, disgusting things he was spouting forth about you to his mate Jez before I slit his throat with the Stanley knife I used for work. One reason for doing this was because I recognised him as the bastard who beat me up in the park. Another was because I didn't want him going near you.

I love you! There I've said it, though I would never have the courage to do so in person. I have loved you from the first moment you fluttered down like an angel into my life. Every waking hour, I love you; I think about you, I crave you. You! I am so sorry for putting you through all the trauma of the death of a boyfriend.

Next was Atkins. I gave him the benefit of the doubt, and he fucked everything up by offering me some Rohypnol to use on you. I helped him to the toilet when he was going to be sick, and he slipped and fell. He started shouting at me, and it was like being back at school again. It all came flooding back, the years of abuse. I bashed his head against the floor to make sure the job was done properly.

Things rather went wrong then. Because I had kept Stuart's mobile, [you can find it taped to the bottom of my bed] I contacted his friend, Jez, the person who I think framed the man called Skinner, who was arrested for Stuart's murder. I got through to his girlfriend and arranged for him to meet me at a certain time and place. After I had done that, I went to Christchurch Park, found Skinner's gang, and told them of my suspicions. I told them of where Jez would be meeting me. I told his girl to make sure he was alone, but they didn't listen. You remember that story in the local paper about the family being killed in a drive-by shooting? That was them, and my fault. I hate myself for that, I really do. Not for Jez's death, but for his girlfriend and child's. They played no part in this.

Then, of course, a more recent turn of events saw me being nearly drowned in a cage of putrid, rotting vegetables. When I disappeared that night, I murdered Nivek's mum and a supervisor, called Steve, and put their bodies in the cardboard-box baler. It's due to be emptied tomorrow, so by the time you read this, you'll have probably seen it on the news.

This brings me up to date, almost. We came to this guesthouse, The Rising Sun, and thought we'd discovered Belgium's answer to Norman Bates, but he turned out to be a sad, lonely man with a mentally-ill, colossal ex-wrestler for a father. Basically, his father broke into Nivek's room and raped him. A blow to the head from his father killed his son, and the sheer weight of the man suffocated my poor Nivek, despite my attempts to fight him off.

I finally managed to get him away from Nivek, and he fell down the stairs and broke his neck. The bodies of he and his son can be found in the basement of the guesthouse. Nivek is in room five, next-door to me. That just leaves Kol'n. At the moment, I'm not sure what to do with him. He found a notebook that I had been cataloguing this series of events in, and I had to silence him. Don't worry, at the moment he is still alive. I really don't want to kill him, but unless I can think of another way out of this...

So that's it. I am so sorry for all I have done; I feel such a sense of remorse that I wish I had never met any of you. To bring this much pain to the people that I love, on you the person that I love the most, is unbearable. I love you, Persephone, and I will always have you with me wherever I am. My plan now is to finish my notebook and disappear into Europe somewhere, where I shall most probably take my life somewhere exotic. I've always fancied going to Venice, or maybe Athens. But I shall have you with me every step of the way, and I'm sure my last glimpse of this world will be of your beautiful face. And all the flawless perfection that I know in its every minute detail.

Farewell, my sweet Persephone,

You will always be in my heart,

Robert

xxx

Well, that is the end of my tale. I am leaving for pastures new on the last train out of this god-forsaken town. I have noticed, as I look out the window, that a bright beam of sun has broken through the rainy sky. Is this an omen? Will things get better from now on? Who knows? I will leave this notebook for whoever gets here first. As for Kol'n, I tried to kill him this afternoon, again, but couldn't go through with it. I held the Stanley knife to his throat, but couldn't draw it across. Maybe I'll try again before I leave. Thank you for reading this, and I am sorry for the people who have died because of me. And I hope that

Jakob's wife if she is still alive, takes pity on him and at least pays her respect to a sad, unfortunate man.

Last but not least, a message to Seph and Thys, just in case this happens to be viewed by your good selves. Thank you for the years we spent living together, I enjoyed every bloody minute of it, every little prank, and every hug. I love you both. See you in the next life.

xxx

God.

EPILOGUE

I don't know where to begin. For those of you who have read this far with the morbid fascination of anyone who reads murderers autobiographies, I hope you have been disappointed. Robert Goddard, 'God' to his friends, was not an evil, cold-blooded killer. He did not have a traumatic childhood and was not influenced by any gothic music or horror films. He was a lovely, warm, caring, beautiful, friendly person, and despite all his faults, I feel honoured to have been his friend.

As for who I am my name is Persephone; I don't think you need a surname, as there is only one Persephone in God's story. His letter arrived the day after the news bulletin about Nivek's Mum's body being found had been reported.

I alerted local authorities in Zeebrugge of the whereabouts of God. They came into the peaceful little guesthouse and carried out four bodies in black body-bags. A rude police officer snatched God's notebook from me and forced me into a car to be whisked away from the crime scene for questioning. I had only been in the town for an hour. As the car sped off, I remember shielding my eyes from the bright sunlight that shone on my face and going over the previous events which led me to be there in the first place.

As soon as I read the letter that God wrote to me, I rushed upstairs to check beneath his bed (the only thing left in the room that he hadn't taken back to his parents' before he travelled). I found Stuart's phone and the pictures taken on the Second World War Memorial in Christchurch Park. God's unconscious body lay bloodied and broken. I sat on his bed and wept for the sixth time since he and Nivek left. My head was full of mixed emotions.

From the moment God went out of my life, as he got in that taxi in the early hours of the morning, I felt as though a part of me had been snipped away. I felt a tremendous sense of loss, and I was overwhelmed by it. It was the age-old cliché that you do not realise you love someone until you have lost him. I had always been close to God, more than the others. We were on the same level, and we understood one another. Well, I thought we did.

It took me a while to take his letter in, and as soon as I read the threat of suicide and the possible harm on Kol'n, I took what money I had in my bank account and my passport and left for Harwich straight away. I had to stay overnight in the port to wait for the first ferry to the Hook of Holland. That is where I did my mourning for Nivek. I had no reason to disbelieve God, but a small part of me, the rational side of me, hoped this was some sick joke. That it was just a ruse to get me to go to Belgium with them.

I did not even register the fact, then, that God had declared his undying love for me. If only he had told me before any of this happened. I wasn't in love with him from the first moment I saw him, but not long after that first encounter, on our first day at college, the more I hung around with him, the more I loved him; maybe not in a sexual way, to begin with, I just loved his humour and personality. Sure he was good looking, even though he portrayed himself to be overweight.

The ferry crossing went by in a blur, I was out on deck most of the time, watching the grey waves and not caring about the rain that stung my face. I almost threw his letter into the sea, in the hope that all this would just dissolve and wash away.

I arrived at the Hook and caught a bus to Zeebrugge, mimicking the boys trip only days earlier. I had a lousy map that I had managed to print off an internet booth in the port. It made my quest to find De Het Toenemen Zon guesthouse harder. Amusingly enough, I actually made myself look like a silly bitch by going into the very pub that the guys had their last night together in. I asked who I now assume was 'Boyd', directions to the guesthouse, to which he hooted with laughter and took five minutes to tell me that it was 'just across the road!' Fucking Aussie wanker!

It was like walking in slow motion when I spotted the guesthouses rusty sign. As I inched closer, I could see that the front door was wide open. In a daze, I entered the house and climbed the stairs. As I went up to them, I noticed a smeared, red hand-mark on the orange and brown wallpaper. It looked like blood, and I could see it was still wet.

The place was so eerily quiet, I dared not to shout or say anything; I was too frightened. I didn't know if... if God were there, whether he would attack me or not. I slowly approached room five and saw what looked like the shape of a person beneath the white sheet. A broken walking-stick lay on the floor. I stopped myself from pulling back the sheet. I was one-hundred percent certain then that this was all real.

I left the room and moved along to the next room, its door was also open. As soon as I peered past the doorpost, I heard a gasp and my heart sank. Lying on the floor, face a deathly pale and clutching at a fast-spreading red patch on his chest, blood on his lips, was God. He looked in so much pain and seemed to take every bit of effort he had to prop himself up against the bed.

"Are you really here?" He asked me in a splutter of blood. I nodded, tears streaming down my face, and rushed down to him. I pulled the sheet off the bed and tried to press it against him to slow the bleeding, but he waved my hand away, shook his head, and said, "No."

I held him in my arms and wept. "Please, let me help you!"

"I'm sorry, Seph," He spat to get out, tears now coming from him "I love you."

I cradled his head, the sheet still in my hand. "I love you too, and really I do. Please, please let me help you. I know what you've done, and I don't care. Even if you go to prison for a zillion years, I'd be there every week to visit you, please!" He smiled, and I could see that special little sparkle in his eyes that always shone when he was exceptionally happy.

"Well in that case..." He said, and moved his hand away from the wound and allowed me to press the sheet against it. I pushed the wad of the sheet against the wound and went to get my mobile phone out to call an ambulance when he fell into my lap.

I pleaded with him to hold on, but as he gazed up at me with his beautiful, blue, sparkling eyes, I could see it was too late. He smiled up at me and held one of my hands. Regardless of the blood, I leant down and kissed him on the lips. God grinned wider, and although it was barely a whisper, I heard him sing, "Heaven, I'm in heaven..." Before the sparkle went out of his eyes.

The police arrived a lot sooner than I estimated, and I soon realised why this was. Kol'n had summoned them. It turned out that God freed him, and as soon as he was free, he stabbed God in the chest with a knife he had secreted about himself as soon as he had read the notebook. The knife had been in the front, left pocket of his jeans and would have been too blunt to cut through the belts had he been able to reach it, but it had a sharp-pointed tip. Kol'n was convinced that God had killed Nivek, but it was proven that he didn't and that Mr Ghysegheem's father did.

There was a lot to take in and hours of questioning.

I never saw Kol'n after we got back to England. I don't think life will ever go back to normal again. I've lost two of my best friends and the man who I cared for most in my life. Every so often, I visit God's grave, and even though his father refuses to, his mother sometimes joins me. I miss him so much, I would rather him be in another country never to be seen again, than where I can still be reminded that he is dead. But I still feel a little piece of him is with me. I often feel him there when I see or hear something he would laugh at; I can almost hear his wonderful laughter in my head. I can still smell him on the holey, old, black and white striped jumper that he always wore, that I snuck from the guesthouse.

This is the end.

VIRGIN AND THE HUNTER

Below, I dedicate an absurdly beautiful poem, by a lady whose name escapes me, to my love, Robert Goddard, and hope he sees the relevance and forgives me for using it.

Always There
Whatever the mood,
Wherever I go,
You are always there.
Like the remnants of a dream,
That never washes away,
You are always there.

The sound of the rain,
Against the window pane,
Reminds me you are always there.

Songs have messages in throngs,
Reminding me,
You're always there.

Every night and day,
Whether awake or asleep,
You're with me when I close my eyes.
Though I may never see the looks on your face,

Or feel the brush of your hair,

You're always there.

Robert Goddard 1984 - 2006

AFTERWORD

This story I completely improvised back in 2006. It was a time when I was finally starting to gain my self-confidence and some self-esteem. The original version of this story had a killer soundtrack to it, but obviously, what with royalties etc.... they have been lost in this version. I just sat down at my computer one day and started typing. That was what I came up with. I hope you enjoyed it.

If you have read and enjoyed this, or even if you haven't, I would be eternally grateful if you were to leave a review on Amazon and/or Goodreads. I don't do this to make money, which is why I always opt for the lowest price tag on my books, but reviews are worth a thousand times more than the money. But the most important thing is your enjoyment.

Thank you for reading.

Author Biography

Matthew Cash, or Matty-Bob Cash as he is known to most, was born and raised in Suffolk; which is the setting for his debut novel Pinprick. He is compiler and editor of Death by Chocolate, a chocoholic horror anthology, and the 12Days Anthology, and has numerous releases on Kindle and several collections in paperback.

He has always written stories since he first learnt to write and most, although not all tend to slip into the many-layered murky depths of the Horror genre. His influences ranged from when he first started reading to Present day are, to name but a small select few; Roald Dahl, James Herbert, Clive Barker, Stephen King, Stephen Laws, and more recently he enjoys Adam Nevill, F.R Tallis, Michael Bray, Gary Fry, William Meikle and Iain Rob Wright (who featured Matty-Bob in his famous A-Z of Horror title M is For Matty-Bob, plus Matthew wrote his own version of events which was included as a bonus). He is a father of two, a husband of one and a zookeeper of numerous fur babies.

You can find him here:

www.facebook.com/pinprickbymatthewcash

https://www.amazon.co.uk/-/e/B010MQTWKK

Other Releases by Matthew Cash

Novels

Virgin and the Hunter

Pinprick

Novellas

Ankle Biters

KrackerJack

KrackerJack 2

Clinton Reed's Fat Illness

Hell and Sebastian

Waiting for Godfrey

Deadbeard

The Cat Came Back

Short Stories

Why Can't I Be You?

Slugs and Snails and Puppydog Tails

OldTimers

Hunt the C*nt

Anthologies Compiled and Edited By Matthew Cash

Death by Chocolate

12 Days STOCKING FILLERS

12 Days: 2016

12 Days: 2017

The Reverend Burdizzo's Hymnbook*

SPARKS*

*with Em Dehaney

Anthologies Featuring Matthew Cash

Rejected For Content 3: Vicious Vengeance

JEApers Creepers

Full Moon Slaughter

Down the Rabbit Hole: Tales of Insanity

Collections

The Cash Compendium Volume One

Website: www.Facebook.com/pinprickbymatthewcash

Copyright © Matthew Cash 2016

Printed in Great Britain
by Amazon